W9-ABS-685

Unrepentant Women

By the same author

The Wife

Unrepentant Women

JUDITH BURNLEY

STEIN AND DAY/*Publishers*/New York

First published in the United States of America in 1983

Printed in the United States of America

STEIN AND DAY *Publishers*
Scarborough House
Briarcliff Manor, N.Y. 10510

Library of Congress Cataloging in Publication Data

Burnley, Judith.
Unrepentant women.

I. Title.
PR6052.U6574U5 1983 823'.914 82-42836
ISBN 0-8128-2914-X

Deep with the first dead lies London's daughter,
Robed in the long friends
The grains beyond age, the dark veins of her mother
Secret by the unmourning water
Of the riding Thames.
After the first death, there is no other.

Dylan Thomas
from *A Refusal to Mourn the Death Of a Child by Fire in London*

Unrepentant Women

1

It was four o'clock in the morning. Deep at the bottom rung of her sleep, a bell tolled. Sarah struggled up through many layers, the weight of heavy waters pulling her back. *Full fathom five thy father lies . . . those are pearls that were his eyes . . . sea nymphs hourly ring his knell . . . Hark, I hear them. Ding-dong. Bell.* In one familiar movement her arm surfaced and grabbed the receiver and her voice, waterlogged, but distinct enough, managed a faint "hello". The telephone: her lifeline.

When Adam was away, as he was now, she kept the magic instrument on his side of their enormous bed round about the level his chest should be, and quite often it spoke to her in his voice from the other side of the world. Adam had a lovely voice. Everyone knew that. He was famous for it. And when it spoke to Sarah it carried warmth and tenderness and regret. Especially when it reached her from a different time zone, another plate of the earth's surface. His telephone calls were the only things in this world she would willingly wake for. Except to make love, of course.

"Mrs Cornish?"

"Yes."

Oh, yes. She knew who she was. Waking or sleeping. Even at four o'clock in the morning.

"Mrs Jacob Cornish?"

It was *not* an overseas call. Her desire to replace the receiver and fall back those fathom five was overwhelming. Gratefully, she began to sink. Down, down, *where no seasons trouble the cold, perpetual midnight. And the womb retains its fruit.*

"Hello – Hell*o* Mrs Cornish?"

"Yes. I mean no. That's my mother-in-law. I'm Mrs Cornish Junior. What is it?"

"This is the hospital, Mrs Cornish."

A cold white slab of steel inserted itself between Sarah and her sleep. The voice continued.

"Do you know where Mrs Cornish Senior can be found?"

"She's sleeping in my spare room," said Sarah.

"Mrs Cornish, Mr Cornish died in his sleep last night."

Died. *Died?*

Long pause.

"But you said – it was a success – the operation. We were told he would recover. My husband would hardly have left the country this morning if there'd been any danger . . ."

"He had a heart attack, Mrs Cornish. In the night. He died in his sleep. Will you make the necessary arrangements?"

"But – I don't know what to do."

"We keep them here, in the morgue, Mrs Cornish. Until arrangements have been made. It is usual to do these things as quickly as possible. We expect you to contact us with your wishes."

The phone clicked. For a few moments Sarah lay in bed in

the darkness searching for the particular soft, warm hollow her body had made while sleeping, and for the sweet, salt, warm, odd animal smell of herself asleep in it, but she couldn't find it. She put the light on and looked at her watch. It was five minutes past four a.m., still dark outside, and she had never been farther from sleep in the whole of her adult life. The room looked strangely altered in the flaky yellow light – her comforting, mellow room. Alone in the warm nest of the bed they called the best bed in the world, she shivered. Outside, a clammy August morning dawned. When would she sleep a sweet uncomplicated sleep again? Instead, a new heaviness settled around her, stiffening her neck, shoulders, spine. Dread. Her eyes felt dry and gritty, her mouth metallic. With a new weariness she got up and rummaged in a drawer for her favourite black lambswool sweater. Old, a bit faded, the elbows out, she had never quite brought herself to throw it away. How right she had been. She had needed it for just this awful moment. She pulled it on over her nightdress, got back into bed and tried to think what to do.

Her father-in-law lay dead on a slab in a morgue, whatever that was like. A large deep freeze, perhaps? A giant fridge? Was he covered with a sheet? Did they cover their faces, too, or only their bodies? Somehow she visualized a row of sculpted shapes under faded blankets, heads proudly exposed, like effigies on sepulchres in the vault of a cathedral, chins up to meet the dark. There was dignity in that. But this was the morgue of a big London hospital in the late twentieth century. Were the dead allowed dignity in such a place?

He had a noble profile, Adam's dad. Patrician. Roman head, white hair, the lot. Had had, that is. A proud, remote and stately man. Would she have to go there alone and see him dead? Would she have to identify the body? (These were the loins which gave my husband life.) She, who had never seen a person dead. And at the end, that plastic sack they gave you with those pitiful possessions: pyjamas, walking stick, wrist watch, coins, an apple. Would they give it to *her* to bear away?

One thing at a time. *One* thing at a *time*. Had Adam arrived in Africa yet? What time was it in Nairobi, now? She ought to know. *In the dark night of the soul it is always four o'clock in the morning.*

She started to make a list: priests, doctors, family, friends. The trouble was she needed the telephone directories, she needed the dialling code book and the address book, but to get them she had to open the bedroom door and go into the hall. This she dared not do for fear she would wake her mother-in-law. Adela slept so lightly. And if she woke, Sarah would have to tell her. Alone, face to face, and before morning. She heard a deep sigh and realized she had emitted it herself. The enormity of the task confronting her settled on her spirit like the night-time quiet settling once again on the old house. She could almost hear the breathing of her small son from his room at the end of the corridor, the tossing of the student who was currently helping to look after him, the grunts and little snores of the old lady, newly widowed, yet unaware. Bereaved. She heard scuffles in the wainscoting, creaking of old floors and window frames, the swish of a car in the road outside. A large, end-of-season fly settled itself inside the lampshade by her bed and proceeded to groom itself with extraordinary precision, endlessly smoothing down, it seemed, a pair of long black gloves. Sarah had just such a pair – unworn – in the drawer opposite, from a trip they had made to Italy. Elegant elbow length gloves in the finest black leather. She watched, mesmerized, as the fly repeated its movements tirelessly. Invitation to the waltz or the beheading? Overhaul for the long distance run? Be prepared . . .

"If he dies, she'll try to kill herself," Adam had warned Sarah long ago. Sarah had never doubted it. Adela had always been the hysterical type. She was also bigger and probably stronger than Sarah, a large, determined woman, and Sarah knew she would need help to cope with her, someone to help hold her down, administer a shot – but who? Her own doctor was on holiday, and she remembered now that Adela's G.P. was, too. Where were they all, now that she needed them? Well, it was August. It would be, wouldn't it? There was nothing for it, she must get the phone books and take the risk. If only she could get herself a steaming hot cup of tea at the same time, but she dare not potter in the kitchen. If only she could tell someone now, and share the burden. But how could you wake anyone, intimate or unknown, in the very dead of night, unravelling their knitted sleave of care? She plucked at the hole in the elbow of her sweater and glared at the telephone resentfully. Why should she be the carrier of doom? Why should she bear the burden of this terrible power? They say knowledge is power and she'd been handed an appalling piece of knowledge. Well, she didn't want it, nor any part of it. It was even possible that it wasn't true. After all, she hadn't seen the body, hadn't looked death in the eye. How strange of the hospital to announce the news at four a.m. when nothing could be done till morning. Why had she been chosen, she who loved them, to shatter all their lives? David, her son, was only seven years old, yet he'd have to learn now that death, which came to hedgehogs and hamsters, could come to grandfathers, too. Adela . . . well, she'd been married for over forty years, almost all her adult life. She was sure to feel her life was over, too. Could you blame her for that feeling? And Adam . . .

The long distance telephone operator, at least, would be awake. She rang the number, chatted about time differences and the hotels in Nairobi, felt better. She placed a call for the morning, rang off, and felt worse. She could predict every nuance of their conversation. He would just have walked in to the hotel lobby. Relaxed. Nonchalant. On top of his job. Adam, world traveller. He'd say "Darling", (delighted) "I've just walked in." He'd mean: how clever of you to welcome me here, like this. He might tell her some detail about the programme he was making, some choice titbit of television madness. She would tell him the news and hear the intake of his breath. His voice would register amazement first, then shock. She could feel the shock register in his body, his need to sit down, absorb it. She waited.

"I'll just turn round again and come home," he said.

"The funeral can't be till Friday."
"All the same."
"Yes. Good."
"I should be there tomorrow night."
"I love you."
"Yes."

She could have predicted, too, the moment he walked through the door smelling of whisky drunk steadily on the plane. His mother went into his arms and they held each other. Sarah saw him thinking he could look at her over his mother's head. She saw him decide to avoid it. He would cry for a week. He had been nine years old when he'd last been close to his father. For a week after his father's death he was nine years old again.

"I couldn't get through this without you," he said, when at last he looked at her.

After the week he went back to work and the episode was closed. For Sarah, it had just begun.

There were many things, that morning, she could not have predicted. Who said daytime is the same as night-time with the light on? Wrong. She could not have predicted, for instance, that the fly which had watched with her through the night would still be there when she switched off the lamp. Black and enormous, somnolent after its vigil, it buzzed unenthusiastically at her. She killed it without compunction, its black body falling with a satisfying fizz-plonk sound into the wastepaper basket.

Nor could she have predicted the effect David's morning hug would have on her, though his small rounded limbs, still heavy and warm with sleep, wound round her no more fiercely than usual. But today she clung to him a moment too long for his patience, comforting herself. How she longed to escape with him to the park, to the ordinary cheerful shopping street, the hurly burly of her office or his school, to the blissful, humdrum everyday! To life. Where she belonged. Her special, full-to-bursting life. What was she doing here with all this heaviness, grief, old age and death? She was Sarah. She was alive.

She was wrong, too, about her mother-in-law. When it came to the dreadful moment, there was no hysteria at all. Adela appeared in the kitchen, dressed as usual in her matching cashmere cardigan and skirt, neatly classic, not a hair of her elaborate upswept hairdo out of place, her gait a bit slow among the unfamiliar furniture of her son's home.

"Now, Mama," said Sarah, "I want you to sit down and I'll make you some coffee."

Adela hovered.

"Please sit down," said Sarah, too fiercely, almost pushing Adela into a chair.

Adela sat.

Sarah put two cups of coffee on the table and sat down facing her mother-in-law.

"The hospital phoned," she said quietly, watching Adela's face. "Daddy died in the night."

Adela said softly: "Oh." A sound like air escaping from a tiny toy balloon. She had her elbows on the table and her beautiful hands were clasped. She swayed once then went astonishingly still, her eyes, as vividly blue as always, bulging slightly.

"Have a sip of coffee," said Sarah.

No answer. She seemed to be in a trance. Sarah watched her, alarmed. My God, she's gone into some kind of catatonic state. What on earth do I do?

She ensconced the old lady in an armchair in the sitting room. Such dignity, said the people who came and went. Such courage. Such strength. Adela remained silent.

They were visited by the vicar, who immediately tried to recruit Sarah for his parish work, and the elderly Jewish doctor from next door, who spoke to Adela in several languages, including her native Polish, which comforted her a little.

Once she asked Sarah suddenly: "What happened?"

"They said he had a heart attack," Sarah told her.

"A heart attack!" echoed Adela.

"After the operation," explained Sarah. "In the night."

Adela returned to her thoughts.

"I saw a light on under the door of your room last night," she said later. "I thought it was odd. I went to the bathroom and I saw the light on in your room, and I thought, something's wrong . . ." And then, suddenly: "Is it true?"

She fixed Sarah with that disconcerting bright blue gaze, undimmed by seventy years, a gaze both childlike and suspicious. Sarah longed to say: No, of course it's not. How could it be? You'll die together in each other's arms. Or, simply, I don't know. They say it is. I'm having difficulty believing it myself. Instead, she held the old woman's gaze as steadily as she could.

"Yes, I'm afraid it is," she said.

Adela lowered her eyes. "It shouldn't have happened like this."

"I know," said Sarah.

"Hospitals. Operations. The miracles of modern science. He should have died at home in bed with all of us around him."

"There was that time..." began Sarah, and saw her mother-in-law nod agreement. "It was just before we had him taken to hospital."

A scene like a death bed scene from one of the Russian novels. An oxygen cylinder at the bedroom door. The heavy old bedroom furniture. The old man, almost pleased to be lying back against lace-edged plumped-up pillows, reassured perhaps, now that the safety of hospital loomed. The three of them: mother, son and daughter-in-law, moving alone or in groups around the old-fashioned apartment, voices low. Time going slowly in a nineteenth century way. Waiting for the ambulance as the three sisters had waited for something to happen that would change their lives. For life to begin. Or end.

Sarah remembered being alone in the silent room, the old man nodding, pale against the pillows, asleep or too tired to talk. She watched him in the mirror, his face, her face, heard an old clock ticking, saw a crowd of photographs – dead family, waiting. It would have been seemly. To die in your own bed with your family around you, peacefully, in your eightieth year. She thought: if I were lying in that bed, would I not prefer to call us round and make a speech? "I am dying, loved ones, dying." In those days you could *know* you were dying. You might even have come to accept it. You could make it a conscious act. You could be in control.

"If this is dying," said Lytton Strachey, "I don't think much of it."

"What is the answer?" asked Gertrude Stein. And, hearing none, asked: "Then what is the question?"

2

It was a week since Sarah had set foot in the street. For seven days and seven nights she had lived the stifling indoor life of *Cries and Whispers*. Now the bright light and sharp sounds of the outside world seemed harsh, bewildering. The bustle, the cheerful purposefulness of people's daily round, had she ever been part of that? Would she ever join it again? She straightened her shoulders, and taking deep breaths, exhaled profoundly, as if to expel misery from her lungs. But although she walked as briskly as usual to her office, her body felt weighted, her shoulders bowed, she felt old. When some workmen whistled at her in the usual way she was amazed and then alarmed and then outraged. Couldn't they see from the size of the burden she carried she was no young woman to be whistled at?

It was only when she walked in to the plate-glass building of the glossy magazine she wrote for, was greeted in the usual way, collected a pile of messages, zoomed up in the lift, that it began to occur to her this new disfigurement didn't show. The usual hysteria engulfed her as soon as she stepped into the pink-walled panic of the seventh floor. Pages were late, features were being re-written, pix had been wrongly cropped. A group of girls from the Art Department trapped her and unfolded a new centre spread for her approval.

"What do you think, Sarah," they giggled. "The first ever nude pin-up of a real live MAN!"

"Do you like him?"

"Do you *want* him?"

"Too many bracelets, perhaps?"

"Is he well enough hung?"

"Depends on how you like beefsteak."

"Medium rare?"

"From now on, I'll take it tough," said Sarah.

She felt curiously detached. Such fuss and fury every month, such certainty the "book" would never get to "bed" on time. It always did. Every month it hit the bookstalls, the word "new" promoting the old problems: how to keep your man, your figure, your bank balance. How to change wardrobe, make-up, career, or heart.

"Oh, Sarah, dear, two more of your Fast Ladies have been pasted-up, and very good they are. We've had to cut, of course."

"Cut? But you know I like to do the cuts myself."

Adrian, the features editor, pursed his lips, smoothed his already smooth white hair and tutted at her. His bright blue eyes remained unmoved.

"Better see Geoff about that. You *were* away."

Bracing herself for the hostility she knew she'd meet, Sarah opened the assistant editor's door and stood on the threshold.

"Geoff?"

The man behind the desk raised his head and his moustache twitched slightly.

"Oh, hello."

His eyes were colder than the coldest reaches of the North Sea. As usual. He cleared his throat, embarrassed by her presence. With what appeared to be a great effort, he produced some words for her.

"Sorry to hear about your, er, father-in-law," he said.

Sarah inclined her head.

"Geoff, Adrian tells me you've cut my two Fast Lady pieces. Could I see the cuts?"

"Too late. They've gone down. You don't want them postponed."

"I don't mind. As long as most of them come out before the book is published. And that gives us plenty of time. Can I ask Ken for the galleys?"

Grudgingly, Geoff nodded. "I suppose so," he said. "These old women are important to you, aren't they?" He looked at her and she thought she saw a gleam of something suspiciously like triumph in his eye. Aha! He had found a vulnerable spot in her, at last.

"Look, Geoff," she said wearily. "Don't let's go over this again. I believe these 'old women' as you call them, will be important to a lot of younger women. I know it's difficult to understand when you've grown up with heroes all around you, from Hamlet, through Biggles to James Bond. But women crave examples, models for their lives. Heroines. People to look up to, and perhaps, to emulate. There's been no one, barring doomed and wicked queens, since Viola and Rosalind took off their doublets and hose and put on skirts again. And they were boys playing girls playing boys."

"Who's for Angela Brazil?" said Geoff.
She shut his door.

Nothing got better, did it? She'd never find out why that man hated her. She just wished, as she'd wished a thousand times before, she didn't react in such a childish way. You'd think, wouldn't you, a girl's insides would toughen up a bit, that after so many years she'd learn to take what they called the rough with the smooth? Yet every time she felt she was eight years old again, and ugly, her too-tightly plaited pigtails pulling at her temples, her woolly stockings refusing to stay up round her skinny legs, a particle of food stuck painfully in the brace on her front teeth. And her eyes stung, as they'd always done, with won't-shed tears. Grow up! So everybody doesn't love you all the time.

She got the galleys from Ken, the chief sub, without trouble, but they didn't show the cuts, and the paste-ups had gone down to the printers. She'd have to phone the printers and get them to give her the cuts word by word on the telephone. Was it worth it, she asked herself. She retreated into the pigeon-hole they called her office, banged the door, a frustrating gesture since it belonged to a flimsy partition, and started telephoning.

The printer's voice intoned each of her words separately, as if they belonged to some ancient mystery language, as yet uncoded. Sarah felt herself getting angrier and angrier as she listened, her spine stiffening at an uncomfortable angle on an uncomfortable chair, the hand clenching the telephone receiver going white around the knuckles. They had cut several jokes she'd grown fond of. They had deleted every belch, every rude or gutsy phrase. They had left in the belly-laughs which had invariably followed upon the ruderies, but these were now rendered meaningless. She took down the details of these mutilations and set to work. It was always possible to cut. Even when one had to take heed of eccentric house style, of elaborate drop caps, unusual column width, and unnecessary running turns, it was surprising how one's copy survived, and survived improved. The subs were so lazy – sometimes they cut whole sentences to avoid a "widow" – one word or one letter left alone on a line. Widows must always be deleted, according to the rules. One had to do the cutting oneself, that was all. There were no short cuts to that. Sarah felt that she owed it to the women she had interviewed to preserve the substance of their words, for through these words they had distilled the essences of hard-lived lives.

"When my husband died," said one old woman, "I wanted to die, too. But I didn't do anything about it. I just went on living from day to day – or rather, existing – and after a while I realized that I was alive, and that what you have to do if you are alive is to live. I mean, not just to exist, but to live. As fully as you can. Life is a gift, after all, and it seems to me sinful not to appreciate it. There are plenty of people walking around dead. You see them everywhere."

Sarah wished she could telegraph these words to both the mothers, Adam's and her own. In neon letters nine feet tall. But what was the use? They sat there, both of them, blinkered in their misery, and she would have to wait, wearily, until they staggered through to their own conclusions. Waiting for elderly parents to adjust to widow or widowerhood, to living alone, being alone, after a life time of mutual dependencies was like waiting for children to grow up and stand on their own feet, only worse. As Sarah's friend Mel pointed out, there was little future in it. For one thing, elderly children were more demanding, more querulous, less endearing than young ones. For another, the chances were they would never make it into an independent old age. Sarah was beginning to despair that her own mother ever would. Dolly had been alone for three years now and there were no signs at all that she could or would adjust. Sarah's father had died three years before, politely, and off-stage, in his deprecating Anglo-Saxon way. Every day since then Sarah had made the same dispiriting telephone call and listened to the same sounds of pain and loneliness and grief. Above all, loneliness.

How are you?
Brave voice: Exhausted.
Are you taking your sleeping pill at night?
Weak voice: Yes. But it doesn't really help. I wake up so early in the morning. Five o'clock. That's my worst time. I lie and listen to the birds, such a cold sound, and I get so lonely and depressed. There's no one breathing in the other bed. We always held hands if we woke up at night. I don't seem to be able to get back to sleep. I lie and wonder what to do all day. I have to be doing something. It's my nerves. I can't sit down. They push me. I mean, you can't get up and clean the silver at five o'clock. I could do the cupboards, but I did them yesterday. I could do the curtains, but I did those last week.
Did you go to the social centre and volunteer?
Warning voice: I don't want to talk about that now.

What happened? Wasn't it any good?

Little girl voice: I can't talk about it, Sarah. It upsets me. I know you think I should get a job. Something to occupy me.

Resentful voice: You're like your father. You believe in work and self-sufficiency. Well, I've tried, but what can I do? I'm not *trained* for anything. It's all right for you, you're young. I went to the doctor about the bruises on my hands. Great dark bruises. They seem to arrive for no reason. And the skin on my fingers is all wrinkled. I thought it was detergent, but it doesn't seem to be. I had all the tests, and this new young doctor asked me all kinds of questions about sex and everything. He examined me everywhere, blood pressure, chest x-rays. He frightened me. He wanted to do a cervical smear, but I wouldn't let him. It hurt when he put that metal screw thing on and I made him stop. You'd think they would know it would hurt when it hasn't been touched for so long.

Bracing herself, Sarah dialled her mother's number, to confirm that she was meeting her for lunch that day, seeing her in her mind's eye as she always did these days, a small figure, alone and helpless against encroaching age.

Poor Dolly. She sat in the light of a big lamp, and she tried and tried and tried to thread a needle. Her hand shook and her eyes watered – even the eye without the cataract seemed blurry today – and the more shaky her hand and the more blurry her vision the more determined she became. To be reduced to this! She who had once been a tiny power house of domestic energy, a five foot nothing generator round which husband and children, schools and servants, meals and holidays and plans revolved, sat alone in all the fury of her frustration, an abandoned child, sixty-five years old. Tears came and she put down her sewing. To be defeated by a needle! She would have to wait until her cleaning lady came. She would have to ask for help. Alone under the fierce light of a standard lamp in the long middle of an empty day she banged her small fists against the arms of His Chair. Nothing went right since he had died and left her all alone. Nothing would ever go right again.

"Just like that, Sarah, just like that," Dolly had said accusingly on the day it happened. "Not a sign. No words for me."

Instinctively, Sarah had put her arms around her, wanting to hold her, this little mother she had always played mother to, but Dolly pushed her angrily away. Clenching and unclenching her powerful small person, she marched furiously from room to room. "Just like that," she muttered. "Just like that."

And now she was condemned to this: eating alone, sleeping alone, coming in to a dark house at night alone. She would never get used to it, never. She wouldn't put up with the life most widows lived, an empty life, a life without men. She'd never succumb to that dreary round of charity work and committees and bridge in the afternoon. Filling their time. It was not for her – she who had never had a moment spare, who had hustled and bustled and got things done. She had never been alone. As a child and the youngest of seven, she had been spoiled and neglected in turn, and her need for attention had become insatiable. Dolly. Small wonder that her childhood name had stuck. You get plenty of attention while your family needs you. All her life she'd been needed. What do you do for attention when you live alone? Well, for a start, you can get your daughter to telephone you every day.

Her lunch time penance confirmed, Sarah turned with relief to the galleys of the next Fast Lady, Mrs Edward Hopper, otherwise known as Josephine Nivison, ex-actress, artist, painter in her own right.

ENCOUNTERS/ENCOUNTERS

"She used to talk to me for hours," said the janitor of the New York studio apartment on Washington Square where Hopper had lived since 1913. "All my lunch hour, sometimes. Well, Mr Hopper was very solitary, you know. Painted away all day by himself. Never came out of his room to join the tea parties she sometimes gave. They drew a line across the floor when she first moved in here, in 1924, she told me. To divide their territory, I think she said, I don't believe they ever transgressed that line. She was lonely, Mrs Hopper. She

ENCOUNTERS/ENCOUNTERS

couldn't share things with her husband. He was apart, somehow. But she loved him all right. They loved each other. "Who'll look after him, where he's gone?" she used to ask me every day in the weeks after Mr Hopper died. You could see she felt it was wrong. She should be with him. She should have gone with him, wherever it was. Even to the other side."

Yet Jo Hopper was never with him, even when they were together, Sarah mused. She was always alone, the picture of loneliness in all his haunting pictures of people alone. Sarah remembered their empty apartment in Washington Square, the bare floor boards stretching away into shadow, the winter-filled skylight. She hoped that the Art Department had got the photographs they'd done there and printed them up to look like Hopper's paintings. She planned a lay-out which would complement the rooms the painter lived in with the rooms he painted, rooms suspended in time, in air: dusty hotel rooms, dingy bars, rundown cafeterias. Jo would be in no hurry to join him. She knew exactly where Hopper was: he was in some tacky cafeteria of the sky.

ENCOUNTERS/ENCOUNTERS

"The funny thing was," the janitor continued, "she'd never looked after him that much when he was alive. Not to my way of thinking. She wanted to show her independence. She was an artist, too, after all, as she told me, often. She had better things to do than cook his meals. One day Mr Hopper drew a cartoon for her showing the cat finishing a meal under the table, while Mr Hopper himself sat starving at an empty table top."

The janitor fidgeted unhappily, twisting large knotted hands between tensed knees. "I wish I hadn't done it," he said. "I wish I hadn't burnt the nudes. She asked me to, you see. She insisted. She must have had her reasons. It was just after he died. He never painted any other woman, excepting her. There was a series of nude paintings. Small, they were, with a sort of sexy power. I still remember them. They were beautiful."

Sarah got through to the Art Department on the internal phone. Edward Hopper? Who he? Oh, yes. Well, we haven't got the trannies yet. Late? We've got our schedule, and we're not late by that. We'll stick to our schedule, and you stick to yours.

She telephoned her best friend Mel, to whom she could confess her fears. There were quite a few of them: all this death might be catching. At the very least it made her feel tired and old. It was possible that she and Mel themselves, though they still thought of themselves as girls, might one day be middle-aged, even old. Everywhere you looked their contemporaries were closing down for the night. Except for the few who were running, or ruining, the country. Every month another egg passed unfertilized down the fallopian tube. Unimaginable intricacies occurred. All those lunar months and human eggs, all those moons pulling all those tides, all that measured activity in vain. She might never have another baby. Time, a concept Sarah had had little time for, seemed important after all. There were biological time-clocks, psychological time-bombs, fuses all set to explode. Doors were built to close, and might one day close on her, in spite of all the jam jars she collected to keep them open. And the worst fear of all? The nightmare? That she, Sarah, the greatest little coper of them all, might one day fail to cope. Mel would have something caustic to say. She always did. But today Mel couldn't talk. She could scarcely listen. Being childless herself, Mel had become a baby minder, and her house was full of children bashing each other on the head.

So Sarah telephoned her friend Jonathan, a playwright and the father of her child.

"I'm surrounded by death and disaster and loneliness," she said. "How're you?"

"Okay. I'm writing a play about death and disaster and loneliness. It's a comedy, I think. How's your series about women without men?"

"A laugh a minute."

"And David? Still into those ghastly jokes?"

"'Fraid so. Do you want to hear the latest? Mmm . . . let's

see. Why is it so hard to open a piano? Because the keys are inside. Why does a boy go to bed with a pencil and paper at his bedside? To draw the curtains when he wakes up."

"Bit clean, aren't they? Nothing ruder, today? I need cheering up."

"There was one which rhymed mum with bum. Very daring. And one about knickers which somehow featured the Queen, but I can't remember how."

"Spoil sport," said Jonathan.

"There was one a small girl told him: 'Ooh, aah, I've lost my bra, I've left my knickers in my boyfriend's car'."

Jonathan chortled. "That's quite nice."

"I believe they get very risqué when they turn seven," Sarah said.

"Are you trying to tell me something?"

"Yes. Next Friday."

"But what can I do?"

"Nothing," said Sarah sadly.

"Now, now. None of that," Jonathan said, briskly. "I may not be there for his birthdays but I celebrated his conception, remember? Did he have much reaction to his grandfather's death?"

"It's hard to tell."

"If he says anything much, jot it down for me, there's a love. It could be useful for the play. I've just heard what Arthur Miller said about why he didn't go to Marilyn Monroe's funeral. 'She won't be there' Miller said. 'She won't be there'."

Next, Sarah ordered groceries, and fruit and vegetables, to be delivered home, and made an appointment for her hair.

Adela telephoned.

"I'm giving Daddy's things away," she said. "They're coming for them tomorrow from Help the Aged. They're very organized, you know. They come with huge plastic bags. I wondered... Would Adam wear a quilted velvet smoking jacket, a paisley silk dressing gown, a practically new dinner suit?"

A smell of old clothes and mothballs and stale *Jean Marie Farina* cologne hit Sarah's nostrils.

"There are things here that are hardly worn," Adela said. "It seems a shame. There's an astrakhan hat."

"Adam never wears hats."

"I know." Adela's voice quavered dangerously.

"Keep what you like best," Sarah said quickly. "And then we'll see. You don't have to get rid of everything at once."

"I'm keeping his watch to give David when he gets older."

"That's nice. I expect he'll come into the smoking jacket one day, too. It will probably be madly fashionable when he's eighteen or so." Sarah thought suddenly of the time when she and Adam used to buy coloured Sobranie cigarettes to go with their clothes. Hadn't Adam had a velvet jacket then? Or was it a brocade waistcoat? Oxford days. Her eyes filled with sudden tears. "But seriously," she said, "don't upset yourself by throwing every thing out today. You can do it gradually."

"I can't bear to see his things hanging there," Adela said. "Do you understand?"

"Of course," Sarah lied. "You must do as you feel."

But she didn't understand at all.

On her way out across the pink carpet of the reception area, she found Adrian on his knees before Sandra, a blonde young person who bore the unmistakeable look of one who had just been "done over" by the beauty department, her sharp Bisto-kid features aged, though not matured, by the zealous application of make-up, the shape of her head unwisely exposed in demonstration of the new "ragged chic".

"Sandra's my new secretary," said Adrian. "Isn't she lovely? She's just dropped her handbag . . . oh, there's a lip-stick," he cried gleefully, diving beneath a desk. "And an eye shadow, too. And there's a dear little brush . . ."

Adrian, their leader, last of the great eccentrics.

Geoff passed by on his way to the pub for the usual liquid lunch. He took in the scene at once. Sarah watched his face, transfixed. There was no one who could signal disapproval so spectacularly, even among the Great Knights of our stage and screen. One eyebrow shot up as his moustache went down, his lower lip twitched convulsively, and there seemed to be a nasty smell under his nose. At the same time his face went puce with embarrassment. It was quite a show.

"How on earth does he manage disapproval and embarrassment simultaneously?" she asked Adrian, when Geoff had gone.

"Lord knows, ducky. Do you think I care?"

At least Geoff's reacting when he disapproves, thought Sarah. It's the only time he shows he's alive. In that sense, Adrian was good for him. An *agent provocateur.* Most of the time Geoff was a walking zombie. *There are plenty of people walking around. Dead. You see them everywhere.*

"Those defences of his are quite something," Adrian admitted. "*À bas les barricades!*"

"I think I'd rather he kept his barricades up," said Sarah.

"We wouldn't take him alive. Behind the defences and the earthworks we'd find the enemy dead."

"If you wait a few moments, Sarah, I'll walk you across Covent Garden," Adrian told her. "Got to be home for lunch, or Adriana won't be best pleased." He arose, flushed, from the floor, presented the girl with her handbag and brushed down the knees of his Prince of Wales check suit. For a moment the girl's stare was riveted to his feet, and a furious natural blush spread under the one so carefully applied, for between the turn-ups of Adrian's trousers and his brogues, lay an expanse of nylon covered ankle, and beneath the nylon glimmered an anklet, a delicate golden chain. The girl's frightened eyes sought Sarah's and Sarah smiled reassuringly. She'd get used to it in time. *We* did!

They swung out across the "garden" together, Adrian's appearance causing the usual disbelief. Passers-by, however, reserved their most suspicious stares for his "companion", Sarah. They must have looked the oddest pair: the girl striding along in a suede-fringed cowboy trouser suit, complete with stetson, the man, tall and distinguished with his neat white head and soberly checked suit, gyrating like the woman he so ardently longed to be. Adrian carried a straw shopping basket over his wrist as if it were a handbag. The short-sleeved shirts he wore under the suit were made at home for him of satin, slippery side next to the skin. Sometimes he sported a padded bra and sometimes went flat-chested. His gloves, grey wool, were like the shirts – proof of a devoted wife, and Adrian wore them long after the fingers were just holes. Each month the basket carried a hopeful tampax, prominently displayed. He swooped as they passed the sites of the morning's vegetable market, adding an uncrushed onion, apple, carrot, cabbage leaf. He was rich, of course.

"Did you inherit, dear?" he asked, stopping at the Savoy to stock up on notepaper and envelopes. "Will your husband be well-orf?"

Sarah hadn't given it a thought. "I don't see how," she said impatiently. "They haven't got much money. I had another row with Geoff. He'll never understand. He doesn't even see why women need to identify with women . . ."

She'd got him. She watched as he tutted sympathetically, "I know. I'll never understand why men like that are employed on women's magazines . . ."

"The trouble is, when I'm confronted by that mug, that frozen face of his – I become as pompous, as patronizing as a man."

Adrian twinkled wickedly. "What did you do, dear, tell him from now on History was to be Herstory? I can just imagine what they're saying in the pub."

So could Sarah: If it wasn't for that silly old poofta, Adrian, the whole damned series would never have got through. Fast Ladies, my foot! I'll never understand why they employ ludicrous old queens on a woman's magazine . . . !

And the joke is, they've got Adrian all wrong, thought Sarah: they think he wants to be a woman so he can make love with a man. He despises men. What Adrian wants is to be a woman so he can make love with another woman.

"Girls who were Famous Queens," said Adrian.

"What?" said Sarah.

"You never listen. It was a book my mother had. A book *her* mother had. There were pictures, too. Poor frightened girls in funny dresses escaping down drainpipes, imprisoned in cells, being beaten, on their deathbeds. It was a book which terrified me. They were the saddest stories ever told. Every one of those girls was murdered, imprisoned, poisoned, betrayed or died horribly in childbirth. And the worst of it is – the stories were all true."

"My cousins passed me down their *Girls' Own Papers* of the twenties and thirties, full of Ovaltinies and stuff about Amy Johnson and Suzanne Lenglen. The serials were about girls who became pilots or tennis champs or vets. If you couldn't fly a plane or knock Wimbledon cold, you could be a vet. It didn't seem to matter that you were female."

"You mean they thought animals couldn't tell: one human being was as bad as another human being? That isn't so, you know. Animals are sensitive to gender in humans . . ."

"The heroines of all the best stories were tomboys. Cut their hair, climbed trees, got into scrapes . . ."

"I was *never* a tomboy," said Adrian firmly.

They passed the flower market. "When I courted Adriana, she was a manicurist at the Savoy," he said. "I used to come to this place at ten in the morning when they were packing up – they open at five, you know – and get whole boxes of flowers for a shilling. Long stemmed yellow roses, she liked best. Pinks – the ordinary garden pinks – were my favourites. They still are. Oh, the smell there in the mornings, all those flowers in an enclosed space. The set for *My Fair Lady* was *exact*, even to the bluish light."

Adrian, last of the romantics.

Sarah had arranged to meet her mother at a restaurant she often used. It had once been a grand old-fashioned dining and dancing place, and Sarah thought Dolly would like it, though it had recently suffered a rather appalling conversion.

Dolly looked round disapprovingly. "It's not what it was," she said. "Daddy and I came here a lot before the war. It was one of our favourites for after theatre supper dances. This and The Trocadero. We used to have curry here sometimes, which was quite a ceremony, served by an Indian in a turban. And then there was a midnight floor show. The Trocadero had the Tiller Girls in theirs."

When they had settled at a quiet corner table, Sarah put two snapshots on the cloth in front of her mother.

"Look what I found," she said.

Dolly took off her glasses and put on another pair. Her hand shook.

"You're trembling," said Sarah.

"I know. It's one of my bad days. This is what I'm like. I can't help it." She peered at the pictures through her reading glasses. One was a wartime picture, Dolly's flushed young face over an old teapot on a little round oak table they'd had. A woman at the centre of her home, certain of her strength, her place. A woman smiling. A woman loving and giving, expecting a family's delight, their greed, their nourishment. For Dolly, each pot of tea had been an offering, and eating a sharing of all the caring, more intimate, even, than making love.

"What a homemaker you are," said Sarah. "Remember that time in the war, in the blackout, when we'd travelled all night across mountains and moors and you had found that ugly little house and made it a haven waiting for us, so that we came in to a small, golden, firelit space, with the tea laid . . ."

"What's this photo?" asked Dolly.

"A photo Adam took. I was cutting bread."

"I can see that. Doesn't look like you."

"No, it looks like *you*. That was the point. Now, what will you have to eat? They have a lovely cold buffet."

"No, I don't want anything cold today. I didn't want to say so, but I've had an upset stomach."

"Well, perhaps some fish?"

"I don't want fish. I have lots of fish at home."

"Well, what would you like? A steak, perhaps. A cut off the joint?"

"Yes, a roast would be the best. I don't get a roast very often nowadays. You can't cook a roast for yourself."

"Now sit back and relax and we'll order some nice food," said Sarah. "I want you to eat a good meal."

There was no plain roast that day. They had steaks. Dolly's was too well done. She wanted to send it back.

"Look mother, please don't, I come here practically every day."

Sarah cut hers in half and passed Dolly the juiciest piece.

"There. Now eat up the vegetables, too. They are beautifully undercooked. You can have these potatoes, with skins on, they're good for you, the vitamins are under the skins."

Her mother chewed sadly. "I'm *very* slow. You'll have to forgive me. It's all very well for you, but after this lunch, I have to go home and be alone again. I shall never get used to letting myself in and knowing that no one's there. I'll take my shoes off and sit down, and rest for a bit, and after a while I'll wonder what to do."

What shall I do now? What shall I do?
I shall rush out as I am, and walk the street

With my hair down, so. What shall we do tomorrow?
What shall we ever do?

Shall I go down to the village and buy a loaf, my loneliness showing, a deformity I cannot hide? I have a contagious disease, and loneliness is its name. I don't go out much. There's so much violence about. The streets are full of cripples. If you look properly, that's what you see. Cripples wobbling along on half a self. The streets are full of limbless people. There's so much violence.

"I don't like the way the world's going," Sarah's father used to say, shaking his head gravely at her as if it were somehow her fault for inheriting the mess. "I don't like what I see at all."

"And now your mother-in-law's a widow," said Dolly unexpectedly. "Would you like me to visit her, dear?" These sudden reversions of role, these moments where her mother decided to play the mother for a change, always threw Sarah. Despite herself, she was touched. How nice it must be to have a mother who was a mother all the time. How comforting. She felt herself sliding with relief into childishness, and pulled herself sharply out of it. She knew from experience that Dolly could not sustain the adult role for long. Besides, she must knock the idea firmly on the head. It could make things worse. The two women had disliked each other in happier moments. Why should they like each other now?

"I never liked her," Dolly went on. "But I feel for her. I really do. Only I know what she's going to go through the next few years." Dolly's eyes grew wet and her glasses magnified the tears. "No one knows what it's like till they suffer it," she said. "Then, they know. Only the bereaved understand." There was bitter satisfaction in her voice. It would come to us all, in the end. She blinked bravely at her daughter. "No one sees me like this except you, Sarah. I keep up a front, like everybody else. And I go on. But my life is useless now. What use is my life? You have a useful life. It will be worse for Adela. She's quite a bit older than me. I wish I were dead."

There was a forward planning meeting after lunch. They'd got to balance the content of each issue between now and Christmas and getting the balance right each month was one of the trickier things they had to do. It was worse than mixing a Christmas pudding: there was always one ingredient you'd been too lavish with, so the mix was too heavy, too sweet, too dark, too light and never seasonal enough. The naughty ingredients this time were old age and death and it seemed to be *Encounters with Fast Ladies* which was spoiling the mix. Or so Sarah's colleagues were determined to think.

"It means I can't use any stories about old people," the Fiction Editor complained. "I even have to keep the serials young and light. At Christmas you must have some Granny and Grandpa stories, not to mention Uncle Scrooge. It won't be like Christmas without them."

"It's the same with the Fashion."

"And Beauty."

"Once we've launched the first of the Fast Ladies with our special issue devoted to the over fifties, I'll be in the same spot," the Features Editor chipped in.

"Over fifties!" exclaimed Sarah. "The Fast Ladies are in their eighties!"

"Well, we can't have elderly fashion."

"Why not? The elderly have to wear clothes."

"Yes, yes. But we can't call them 'elderly' or 'old'."

"Old is a three-letter word."

From the end of the long conference table the Editor interrupted.

"We just avoid those words. They're against our image."

Sarah laughed silently into a plastic cup of peculiarly nasty instant coffee.

"And as for grislies, those horror stories of our time" said the Features Editor, "how I lived happily to a hundred though deaf, dumb, blind, one-legged and a dwarf – they give me the creeps – you know what the Public is like. If it doesn't get fed its fair ration of grislies, each one grislier than the last, it Rebels. It Writes In. It Complains."

Sarah looked at Adrian for support. He was studying his fingernails. "You've got a fabulous feature series on birth, haven't you? The one where the photos were taken from inside the womb?"

She looked round the table, from face to closed face, from hand to clenched hand, from foot to frenetically tapping foot. Brows were furrowed, spines twisted, pencils chewed. Doodles grew steadily more vicious.

"You don't have to counteract the Fast Ladies," said Sarah. "You've got the whole thing wrong. These women may be old but my pieces about them are not gloomy or downbeat. They're upbeat, heartening. They're about people who have lived full lives. They are heartening in the same way as the grislies are heartening. Life was tough, but they 'smiled through'."

Geoff looked shrewdly round the table, too. "You were all very keen on the series when Sarah first mooted it," he said levelly. "I seem to remember that *I* was the only doubtful one."

A babel of disputing voices rose as unhealthily as the cigarette smoke in the airless room. Every move he makes carries a warning. Clever Geoff, thought Sarah. He never misses one. She buckled her chain mail vest on and plunged into the fray again. "We're all afraid of old age and death," she said. "But you underestimate the readers. That's dangerous. You patronize them. Don't. We patronize readers at our peril."

Someone put on a Woody Allen voice: "I'm not afraid of dying," he said, "I just don't want to be there when it happens."

"A third of our readership is over fifty." Sarah continued. "An unknown percentage older than that. But you can't be more than fifty in a women's magazine. Not in print, at any rate. It's never been heard of!"

"She's right," Adrian said, at last. "Younger people may want to read about older people, sometimes." He patted his silvery hair. "It's not always the other way round."

"We wouldn't know, anyway," said someone else. "Those market research samples are far too small."

"Exactly," said Sarah, "so let's be straight about it. All we've got to go by is our own gut reaction. I just want to point out what taboos they've become, ageing and death, since Victorian times, replacing all the old taboos on sex. I was reading some volumes of this magazine from a hundred years ago. My God, the morbidity makes your hair stand on end. How to mourn, how long to mourn, how long it was proper to wear black and when it was seemly to go into violet. How to make fashionable mourning rings, lockets, brooches, from locks of the lost beloved's hair; how to frame photos in black, to border your notepaper black; how to make special mementoes for the children you'd lost. Tombstone engravings. Tombstones and the care of. What flowers to plant on the beloved's grave. Now *that* was seasonal. Oh, it goes on, I tell you. Knit yourself a cosy little black shroud for Christmas. They went to one extreme and we've gone to another – we're hooked on perpetual youth, with sex as the secret elixir. There's nothing we can't say about sex nowadays, unless it's that the elderly enjoy it!"

"Or that anyone's happy without it," said Adrian.

"Our readers have tough lives," said Sarah. "They don't always want to read about bright young things having a nicer time than they ever had; girls who are younger, prettier, luckier than they. That depresses them. They want to read about women like themselves, women who've had it tough – but survived. That gives them hope, and the courage to go on. They think – *She* did it, against all odds. So can I!"

Rushing from the meeting to pick up David, Sarah experienced a familiar surge of guilt. This afternoon's battle had meant arranging for her child to stay an extra hour at a schoolfriend's house. Had it been worth it? Were her priorities all wrong?

"Will Daddy be home?" asked David, playing bears and squares on the paving stones.

"Yes. But he's working. I think he's got a meeting."

David: (at seven) "So – what else is new?"

Adam had got stuck into work again with tremendous relief and work, of course, had restored him to his normal self. He opened the door, gave them a bear hug each, and beamed at them. His tie was off, his hair ruffled, his face flushed, and behind him through a half-opened door, the buzz and smoke of his meeting. So the king enjoys his own again!

She gave David his supper in the kitchen and started getting him to bed, which involved a story, a song, and a prayer, not to mention his special stripey flannel, which could be folded or crushed, damp or dry, but which had to be in bed with him before he would sleep. Lately, he had taken to singing the song himself, having recognized that Sarah's singing voice was not the most beautiful thing about her. The prayer resembled nothing so much as an ever-growing list of requests to a formal court of appeal.

Adam's meeting broke up in time for him to take over the last two items in this show.

"Thank heaven the little blighter didn't mention Grandpa, except in his prayers," he said to Sarah later. "What do we say when he asks us where he's gone?" He was sorting out the contents of his briefcase, which was organized like a general's tent before battle. "I've got some interesting ratings to show you. Secret, of course. God, what a relief it is to be back at work! Even the treachery and the hassle seemed amusing. There are some quite sinister developments. Documentary versus Arts Features, as usual." He riffled through his specially marked copies of the *Radio Times* and *TV Times*. "I'll have to watch the competition in," he glanced at his watch, "fifteen minutes. Will dinner be ready in time?"

Sarah prepared grilled trout and tossed the salad. Adam was on a diet. They sat down to eat.

"There were some nasty remarks in the Bar, disguised as jokes, about the budget for my African programmes. I think they came from the Senior Common Room. I don't like it."

"Mm. I thought it would be great being back, too," she said. "But I had an awful day. They'd cut my copy crudely, so I had to re-cut. It ended up shorter, but better. Why they hire subs who can't sub I'll never know. And I had my mother, in a less than cheerful state, for lunch. Oh, and your mother phoned. She wants to know if you'd wear any of your father's old clothes?"

Adam shuddered. "I hope you said 'no'. You must be careful, Sarah. The two old bags in one day is far too much. They'll get you down. Can't you stagger them a bit?"

Sarah looked at him sharply, but he had left the table and was busy marking up a time-sheet.

"Do you have any suggestions about how I can do that?" she asked drily. "Like getting my husband to cope with his own mother himself, for instance?"

Adam smiled. That remote, somewhat lordly smile she'd seen so often on his father's face. It wasn't a smile at all. Adela had tried to explain it to her once.

"People think they're smiling," she'd said. "They look as if they're smiling. But it's just their mouths, you know. The whole family's like that."

Sarah stacked the dishes while Adam fiddled with his TV

set, adjusting the colour and the contrast with special knobs he'd had fitted by someone from the studios.

"You will phone my mother for me, won't you? Even if you have spoken to her once today? She expects that good-night call just at the moment."

Sarah clattered about with coffee cups.

"In a minute."

Adam mimicked her, as he always did when she put things off.

"In a minute, in a minute." Then added, disarmingly, "I'm sorry you have to, but you know how it is. I can't talk to her. And I need to know she's all right."

He settled down to watch the nicely adjusted box.

"It's now that the guilt has settled in, I can't stand it." Sarah said. "I can hear the crackling of the funeral pyre in the background all the time. And I have to rescue her from it. Every day."

"I know," said Adam absently.

Eventually, Sarah went into their bedroom and made the call.

"How are you?"

In tones of one who says "Why am *I* alive?" Adela said: "How should I be?"

And after the midnight movie, yawning and stretching on the way to bed: "Did you phone my mother?"

"I did."

"How was she?"

"How should she be?"

3

Sarah picked up an advance copy of the magazine and read the first of her *Encounters with Fast Ladies* to appear in print. This month, said the blurb, we introduce the first of a series of portraits of remarkable women. Born in the last decade of the nineteenth century, they have lived, loved, suffered and survived. Rebels, pioneers, outlaws, exiles, they were shunned by polite society, denounced, betrayed. Now, after revolutions, two world wars, the rise, fall, rise and fall of the feminist movement, they bear witness. They are legends, heroines, mirrors for ourselves – and lonely old women. Sarah Cornish reports.

Encounters with Fast Ladies 1.

They had set the piece quite well, Sarah noticed. There was plenty of space round those grey column inches and the pictures were clearly reproduced. Being as vain as the next old lady, Julia had refused to be photographed so the feature was illustrated by a classic profile drawing done by Augustus John when she was very young and in Paris, and a war-time portrait in oils, by her second husband Lawrence Gowing, beautifully evocative in mood, both of the woman and of the period. She sits in front of a fireplace in which no fire glows, reading a book.

ENCOUNTERS/ENCOUNTERS

There was a sudden summer storm the day I visited Julia Strachey for the first time. She lives marooned in an eyrie at the top of a ruined house on the Soho/Bloomsbury border. Percy Street, to be exact. There are several flights of collapsing stairs. I arrived breathless and sodden, my beige linen suit ruined. My shoes squeaked. My hair dripped. Julia was pale and elegant, a tall thin lady somewhat aloof in manner. Surely there had been some mistake? This woman was not "old". A smell of dust and rot permeated the tiny crowded room, accentuated by the smell of my jacket now drying by a small gas fire.

"The mice nibble everything," Julia said, removing a dish of cheese biscuits ragged round the edges. "What will you drink?"

Some sickly sweet sherry and a bottle

of Scotch stood by a pitcher of water clearly drawn from a well near Garsington in 1916. I could see no ice.

"A whisky would be nice," I told her.

"Water?"

"Rather have it neat, please. If I may."

"Oh, I say," said Julia, gleefully. "I think that's awfully fast."

She fixed me with a watery young eye and I saw that what had seemed aloofness was a vagueness of expression which accompanied movement, action, dealings with the practical world of drinks and jackets, cheese biscuits and sudden rain. Nothing could be less vague or less aloof than the attention she focused on words, ideas, people, or conversation. Virginia Woolf must have been much like that if you knew her. Julia had, of course, and supplied me with a thumbnail sketch.

"I once watched Virginia walking down the road and you know it was as if her body was nothing to do with her at all – it was all over the place, uncoordinated, not pulled together. She did not seem to inhabit her body. I was watching a person who was quite unaware of her physical manifestation. Unaware, probably of being there in that street at a certain time on a certain afternoon. Of moving one foot in front of the other, or carrying a bag in one hand. The real Virginia Woolf was elsewhere. And yet she was intensely concerned about her appearance. She worried a great deal about clothes – the diaries tell us that. Perhaps because they adorned or presented someone who was not she – and over whom she had little or no control? What a mystery it all is."

Julia stares out of the window. The bustling street below is full of promises – a Greek dinner, a genuine Georgian doorknob, a freshly roasted quarter of coffee beans, Percy Street can offer all of these, and more. But these enticements are four floors down and a continent or two away from Julia. She never sets foot in the street. How can she? All those stairs to climb again! And she dare not fall nowadays, or risk breaking anything. "My bones don't seem to heal anymore," she says.

We are in another world, that's clear. What year is it? It's 1905, I think, the year Julia was sent "home" to England. She sees herself on the deck of a huge ship, a tiny figure in sailor-collared frock, hat and ribbons, surrounded by wicker hampers, trunks and turbulence. It is the last time she remembers being happy.

"Then my parents kissed me and left and the ship sailed. I was alone in the captain's care. I was banished. From everything. From warmth and sunlight and colour. From my ayah, and from my kitten and from my playmates. From the sights and smells and sounds of everything I'd known. From India. But worse. (Countless analysts explained this to me as I lay on countless stiff uncomfortable horsehair couches in Paris, Vienna, Berlin, Baden-Baden, comfortless and inconsolable.) Worse than banishment or exile. I had been abandoned. How could my parents love me if they sent me away? I had been rejected. I must have been a very bad child to have been so severely punished. Clearly I was unlovable."

Julia plucks mournfully at the frayed edge of an Omega workshop cushion. "I simply cannot fathom it, you know. I *was* pretty, in those days, and they *were* fond of me. I got a lot of attention in India. I remember it. They played with me. They were endlessly picking one up and putting one down. And then they sent one away. How could they do it? At four years old! Yet everybody did it. It was the wisdom of the day. India was bad for the health of English children after the age of four; if they stayed, the climate would ruin their health. England: a healthy mind in a healthy body. The English spirit: something bred by breathing that bleak damp air in your formative years." She shivered and pulled her cardigan together over her concave breast. "I've never been warm again."

"I was to stay with Alice Russell, Bertrand Russell's mother. She 'boarded' me for several years and I hated her. She was really a horrid woman. Cold and severe and altogether unloving and she didn't *like* me. Oh, Alice was foul to me. I remember those horrible rooms in the attic of her Bayswater house with bars across the windows for the safety of children – or to stop them from jumping out. Those gloomy houses the Stracheys and their friends inhabited, like the one my uncle Lytton grew up in at Lancaster Gate, those tall, narrow, confining houses. Is it any wonder that we painted everything in sight when we grew up? Grabbing the exotic wild-beast colours of the Fauves for our Omega workshop, living with gaily painted furniture all around us, with brilliant rugs and pottery and brightly coloured clothes? But in the beginning, and I suppose in the end," said Julia, "one is a Strachey. I tried and tried to shake it off, but it sticks. All Bloomsbury was a reaction to those late Colonial values, an attempt to shake them off. And now Bloomsbury sticks. School was the usual hell, of course, and one was bright, of course, and the despair of teachers because most of the time it meant less than nothing."

"How did you survive?"

"I can't think," said Julia, the classic brow furrowed as she stared at her narrow feet clad in classic beige courts in triple A with the medium high heel chosen by women who are used to being taller than their men. "One endured. And then, I think of what David Garnett said in answer to a similar question. 'I suppose one was always in love,' was what he said. And that got one through everything. The sheer intensity, the hell of those schoolday loves blotted out the everyday kind of hell.

"During the school holidays I stayed with different members of the family and drove them all mad. A long, nervous, melancholy streak of a girl who used to sneak into the drawing rooms of those gloomy houses late at night, find the piano in the dark, and pick out, sometimes beat out, Black music, into the small hours. Jazz. I was crazy about it. Played it pretty well. Still do. I play by ear, and I'd strum on any piano, any time I could. The Stracheys have no ear for music at all. They were stone deaf or tone deaf all of them. They were all kinds of deaf, actually. They'd concentrated so hard on their precious intellects, a great deal had gone by the board. And you've got to remember that this was in the darkest days of the war, when all the men and boys we knew were in the trenches."

"What happened then?"

"Oh, yes," – nervous flick of the wrist. "I went to Paris. I left school, and I refused to go to Oxford or Cambridge, and I took myself off to Paris. Not to the Sorbonne, either. I mooched about Montmartre, which was full of English artists, and I strummed a bit on club pianos and I became a mannequin. It seems I was the right shape. They wanted us straight up and down, you know. Anyway, I supported myself and quite soon I became known as 'the English girl' in the French fashion houses. I wore all the new clothes: Schiaparelli, Chanel, people you wouldn't have heard of, Poiret, Paquin, Worth. Clothes were all part of the post-war revolution in art and we were all pioneers, the elegant mixing quite happily with the Bohemian. The ballet linked all elements, fashion and art, music and design. Diaghilev saw to that. I was probably wearing a couture outfit when Augustus drew me, though you can't see it. Augustus always looked like Augustus, of course, and his women and children often went barefoot.

"Unlike those hectic schoolday passions, which were seldom, if ever consummated, I couldn't trust any adult enough to love, in case I was rejected again, but that didn't seem a problem at this time. For one thing, so many men had been killed in the war, and so many wounded; for another, so many of the young Englishmen I knew were homosexuals. With them you could give and receive a guarded kind of love, which suited me. I didn't know then there were other ways you could be betrayed.

"My first husband was the sculptor Stephen Tomlin, with whom I lived an English country house life. I described it in *An Integrated Man*. I'd had a critical success in 1932 with *Cheerful Weather for the Wedding*. Years later, I met a much younger man, Lawrence Gowing, and we married and I wrote and he painted and the *New Yorker* took me up and naturally after a long time he met a younger woman and they're married now with children and I visit them a lot.

"The trouble is, I'm not well, anymore, you see. I can't eat, and I'm getting thinner. I was always thin, but the doctors are worried: my bones are so brittle. I get depressed. And I get grumpy too. It's all right when people can call you sardonic, but not when you're bad-tempered all the time. But I'm trying to work: writing about my childhood, as befits old age. It isn't going well." A bleak expression sits incongruously on this face made for satire, for the thrust and parry of iconoclastic wit.

"Why can't you eat?"

"I don't know. Even if you brought me mangoes for breakfast and sprayed the room with the smells of morning in an Indian hill station, I wouldn't be able to eat."

Her short novel, *Cheerful Weather for the Wedding* is like that Vuillard painting on the wall, all billowing curtains and "telling" detail, and it, too, will outlast her. How English her work is, and how much a product of that trauma on the ship so very long ago. You recognize it, don't you? That reticence which shadows so much of English writing.

That determination not to confront deep feeling, but to observe obliquely, through a glass darkly, through the eyes of a child narrator, through a veil of leaves or a vale of tears. Julia's book tells the story of a wedding through the details of the preparations: furniture being polished, flowers arranged, the *fuss*. One doesn't, I mean, one wouldn't, describe the couple, would one? Or discuss such questions as who loves who – or why?

Trophies crowd her space. One of Rodin's sexiest bronzes, the sinuously writhing *Amor Fugit*, given to Julia by the artist himself, of course, weighs down a minute corner table, its passions too big for the little room. There are some lovely, tranquil, Gowing landscapes. (Did they picnic by this stream? Did they watch the light change in this valley?) And there is Carrington's last painting, yes, the one she left unfinished the day she went out and shot herself. Is this old age? To suffocate in memories?

Steam rises from the gas fire and the smell in the room is compounded now of biscuits and whisky and mouse droppings and dust and dry rot and wet rot, the stench of painful past. Julia sniffs disdainfully and pours another Scotch.

Downstairs, the purveyors of the food of five continents go about their business, unaware of her existence. Sad and sardonic, the lady who can't eat sits by her gas fire on this damp summer night, growing thinner, growing bitter, still grappling with what happened to her on that ship, still four years old and a long way from home.

4

The next day was editorial conference day: one issue of the magazine would be put together in detail, complete with finished layouts for picture spreads, titles for everything, and immortal selling lines. They worked eight weeks ahead, and often believed themselves to be in October when it was sweltering summer outside. Titles, selling lines and cover lines were composed on the spot at this meeting, everyone vying to be the sharpest, funniest or most vulgar quipster in the room. Once the cover picture was chosen, the seal was set on the theme of the issue, if there was a theme. Decisions at this meeting were final. It was a once a month marathon, an endurance test: they were all bound to stay until the issue was complete, down to the page of star signs at the end. Time was when they had broken for lunch and gone to a nearby wine bar, but the Editor had got fed up with them coming back drunken and jolly and settling down to an afternoon of rude jokes instead of sober autumn knitting titles, or clever limericks instead of "She had waited all her life for this moment" and other unforgettable fiction selling lines. Nowadays, they had cold food brought in half way through.

Sarah never looked forward to conference day. There was a sense of imprisonment, as well as of heightened competition about it. By half-time people were laughing raucously with relief that their own survival strategies had not come unstuck. By mid-afternoon everyone was growing weary and starting to form gangs or little groups to plot, in sign language or in under-the-table notes, how to knock out the rival gang before the end of school. Besides, Sarah reckoned she had won some points yesterday. They would all be after her. They were.

"Well, of course, we were going to have the Queen Mum on the cover this month," the Editor opened. "But what with the cover story and the piece about ladies-in-waiting that goes with it, half the magazine would be for older readers. These *Encounters with Fast Ladies* are so damned *long*." He turned his toes inwards under the table as he said this, and unconsciously covered his balls with a double page beauty spread.

By noon they had managed to find teeny-bopper knitting, virgin brides, and something called "Pigtails out of School" – a hair feature – to correct the balance towards the young. By two o'clock they were working on cordon bleu cooking for the kindergarten when the phone rang. The Editor made a face and picked it up.

"Sarah, it's for you."

Everyone looked at Sarah. It was the unwritten rule that you did not have telephone calls put through at conference. Her heart beating audibly, Sarah took the call.

"I'm sorry," said the girl who was taking her messages – there were no secretaries for special features writers – "but an old lady phoned for you. A neighbour of your mother-in-law's she said. I didn't want to interrupt you in conference but it sounded urgent. It seems old Mrs Cornish fainted and was found unconscious on the bedroom floor. She's recovered now, but wants to know if you can come."

"Of course I will," Sarah said. "And don't worry. I'll phone back myself to reassure her that I shall."

She turned to face the room. "I have to go. I'm sorry," she said. "It's Adam's mum. She was found unconscious on the floor."

"Poor Sarah," said Adrian, almost inaudibly.

Fourteen pairs of eyes condemned her.

"Really, Sarah," the Editor said. "The Conference *is* the Conference. You're needed here."

The others joined in with alacrity.

"You've been off a lot lately."

"It isn't even your own Mother, for God's sake."

"It's not your problem. Why can't your husband deal with it?"

"I mean, everybody's parents die."

Sarah picked up her files and her handbag and made for the door.

"Shall I apologize that it happened in conference time?" she said. "That's what you'd like, isn't it? People should choose a better time to be ill, or to faint, or to die. It's the intrusion of private affairs into public life you can't bear, isn't it? I've crossed the great divide. The split. Well, I'm here to tell you there ain't no divide and it's a phoney split you've decreed." She was shaking badly but she made herself go on. "Oh, it makes your working life a whole lot easier if you separate it from emotional life. But we're not building oil rigs or artificial lungs. We're not running the Stock Exchange. What's happening to me today is supposed to be our subject: family matters, the responsibilities of wives. We're lucky because we don't have to be schizoid. We can use our emotions in our work. It's not a bank."

"Sometimes I wish it were," she heard Geoff say as she closed the door behind her.

Sarah went back to her office past the vending machine. She found a coin, inserted it, selected coffee with milk, no sugar, pressed the button. Waited. Nothing happened. She banged the machine. Nothing happened. She kicked the machine. A fountain of boiling brown goo gushed out at her, splashing her files, her skirt, her shoes, burning her hands and feet. She shrieked, cursed, and retreated to the ladies' room.

Soon I'll be reduced to howling in the loo, she thought.

Back in her cubby hole she telephoned Adela.

"Darling, you don't have to come," the old lady said. "I'm all right. I had a fright, that's all. Everyone's been so kind."

"I've got to find someone to pick David up from school," Sarah told her. "Then I'll be straight over. It'll take about an hour."

"They've given me brandy," Adela giggled. "Imagine! In the afternoon!"

Let's see now. It was twenty-to-three and David's school came out at half past three.

She telephoned home. No answer. Of course, the student au-pair was out at her English lesson. She started to telephone Mel, then stopped. How could Mel pick David up and leave all those other children unattended? Reluctantly, she dialled the TV company and asked for Adam's office. She got a cool, efficient female voice. "He's dubbing. Yes. I think he's in G. Hold on." A buzz. A click. Cut off. Sarah tried again. "Dubbing theatre here. Yes. Just a minute." Terse and immersed, Adam came on the line and said, "Yes?" Gabbling as nervously as if he was a stranger, Sarah explained.

"I'm dubbing," he said. "I've got the theatre till six." His voice was a perfect mix of patience and desperation. "Look, you know what it costs."

It was ten minutes to three. Well, she'd just have to take David with her, that's all. She supposed she would find a way to shield him, once they got there. There was always television.

Everything in Adela's house was arranged in pairs. Two chairs by the dining table, two high-backed armchairs side by side in front of the television set, two towels on the bathroom rail, two rigid old-fashioned bedsteads pushed together. There were even two Chinese vases on the mantelpiece. When Sarah rang the bell, Adela was sitting transfixed in front of the television set. She always had the volume on full, so as Sarah followed David through the door she heard the commentary clearly:

"Everyone is very concerned this long hot summer at the fate of the widowed swan on the London Serpentine, whose mate was so brutally murdered by vandals – in fact, decapitated, six weeks ago. Swans belong to a small group of creatures who mate for life, that is to say that unlike most of us humans, they are naturally monogamous. The bereaved swan has been pining away now for six weeks. She will not eat or drink or groom herself. She will not circulate. All attempts to introduce her to another mate have failed, and attempts by the London Zoo to feed her intravenously have proved inadequate. It has now been suggested that she be removed to a health clinic, or bird sanctuary, where she will be put under sedation, fed by injection, and watched carefully. However, it must be said that her condition has deteriorated so far that it may not be possible to save her."

Adela switched off the set and turned to Sarah, her face a mix of tragic and triumphant.

"I'd love a cup of tea," said Sarah.

"Any biscuits?" asked David.

A girlish eagerness replaced the stark expression.

"Darlings, of course."

Someone needed something in her house. Adela shot into action. China rattled, a tray was set, the kettle hummed. David explored the old-fashioned rooms with fascination. It was some time since he'd been here.

"Smells funny, Mummy," he said. "It smells of oldness. May I have the telly on again?" He switched to his favourite channel, and sat on the floor to watch, a box of biscuits at his side.

Sarah wandered around the cluttered rooms. There were snapshots and portraits and pictures everywhere. Life would consist of memories from now on. Adela appeared with the tray, her hand steady, her movements brisk. She put the tray down decisively on the table and poured two cups of tea.

Sarah looked carefully at Adela. Had this woman been

unconscious on the bedroom floor two hours ago? Adela read Sarah's mind.

"I'll show you what happened," she said, leading Sarah to the marriage chamber. It had a ghostly look. She'd shrouded one of the two beds which lay side by side as one, in an old sheet. She'd done it in such a way that pillows, blankets, bolsters looked sinister, the shapes of ill-formed bodies. She'd shaded the lights with scarves and covered the mirror completely with a shawl. The curtains were drawn across the summer evening sky. The wardrobe doors hung open.

"You see," Adela said, pointing to the empty space within. "All gone. I gave them away. They came for them all this morning, as they said they would. Excepting these. The ones I kept for Adam." She pulled open a cupboard and a suit of clothes on a hanger with a hat atop swung violently, back and forth with a terrible creaking sound.

"The doors of this cupboard were open. I looked up and this suit was swaying in the breeze, with the astrakhan hat on top. I thought for one moment it was him. He'd come back. I felt sure he would, you know. I expected it. I mean, I know he isn't dead. Then I fainted."

"Who found you?" Sarah asked.

"The window cleaner. He saw me through the window, though the curtains were drawn, like this. They're thin you see. And he told the porter. And the porter came up. Then one of my neighbours did, too. Now for the first time I feel what it is to live alone. What would have happened, Sarah, if they hadn't found me? How long would I have lain there, on the floor, alone? Oh, there's something for you, here." She took down a hat box, a round satin-striped affair, and opened it.

Inside was a white velvet pill box hat trimmed with a black sequinned butterfly and a lot of black veiling. Adela stared at it in rapture.

"Try it on, darling. I'm sure it will suit you. It's so modern it could have been made today."

Sarah went into the hall to try the hat on before an unshrouded mirror. How flattering veiling is, she thought. Adela followed her.

"That hat! If you only knew the story behind that hat! How I wanted it! How I saw it from the bus in a window of a smart shop in Park Lane. How I came home and told Daddy all about it and he made such fun of me. 'It won't be there tomorrow' I wailed. 'I should have got off the bus and bought it then. Tomorrow it will be gone.' 'What a stupid person I married,' Jacob shouted. 'What a child! If the hat's not there tomorrow you'll get another hat.'

"As soon as I could next day I hurried to the shop, but the beautiful hat was no longer in the window. My heart fell as I went in and described the hat. The assistant stared at me, and went and fetched the Manageress. 'Are you Mrs Cornish?' I nodded. 'Your husband was here this morning. He asked us to keep the hat for you.'" Adela sighed. "I lived with that man for forty years and I don't think I knew him," she said. "He could be romantic, like he was about the hat. And he could be horrid. He was so remote. Do you think you know Adam?" Sarah blushed and wondered what she could say, but Adela hurried on.

"There was the time I'd provoked him by threatening to leave and he yelled at me: 'Okay, divorce me, but I'll keep the child. You needn't worry. I'll look after him. I'll send you his *kaka* every day so you can see how much he's done and if it's enough or not enough. I'll pack it nicely, don't you worry, and you can be the judge!'

"And there was the time when I waited and waited for him in some little German spa. Salzuflen, I think it was . . . we'd not been married long. Imagine! A girl in her twenties, in those days, alone in such a place, a newly married girl, fending off other men. Talking of her husband. Waiting for her husband. I waited a whole week for him there, on his instructions. Seven long days and nights. I suppose he thought it was a holiday. And when, at last, he came, he didn't look at me, he looked around the room and found it too small. 'It's a single room,' I explained. 'They had no doubles free.' 'Well, I can't sleep here. The sofa's much too small. I'll go to an hotel.'

"I made a scene. I cried. I picked a quarrel. 'Most men would sleep on the floor to be near the woman they loved,' I told him. Jacob was unperturbed. He went and found himself a good hotel. He ate a hearty meal. (I couldn't eat). And he slept, I'm sure, as usual, like a log."

Adela wandered from room to room of the large old-fashioned mansion flat, fingering photographs, picking up objects and putting them down again, and Sarah trailed her, still wearing the pill box hat.

"I never should have married him," Adela said. "I knew it was wrong. I had my chances. Once I was even courted by the celebrated 'Faust'." Sarah blinked hard and shook her head and for a moment the room spun: piano, portraits, clocks, vases in pairs, faces and places, yesterday, yesteryear. Had she heard correctly? Adela went ruthlessly on.

"Faust was the mayor of the small Polish town where we lived, fifteen minutes on the train from Cracow. He was called Faust because he had knowledge and power. He was also a painter, quite a good one, and a notorious anti-semite. All the Jews were afraid of him. Faust saw me in the park and followed me.

"'I must see you,' he informed me. 'I am the Mayor.'

"I put my nose in the air. He followed me.

"'I'll manage to meet you, you'll see. I am the Mayor.'

"A local boy passed and took his hat off to me, so Faust asked the boy to introduce us.

"'You are like a mountain fern, like an orchid, a rare plant,' he said. 'Your profile is roman, your eyes are periwinkles. I should like to paint you. Ask me to your house.'

"I can't," I told him. "We are Jews. It is true my family would be impressed because you are the Mayor, but your views on the subject of Jews are too well known."

"'So! I hate the Jews and I love you,' he told me.

"I was weak. I was flattered. I used to meet him. But I never let him paint me and I never asked him home.

"Our meetings were innocent of sex, of course. We went for a tea or a coffee. We went for a walk. There was no 'sleeping' for nice girls in those days. We flirted but we did not 'sleep'. I don't think it would have occurred to us."

She held out a faded snapshot. Sarah stared at it.

"I should have married *him*." Adela said.

Poland, 1922. A park. A willow tree. A bench. A lake. Two boys in a boat, their faces blurred a little, and – vividly – a girl, her head thrown back, laughing. Blonde hair falls around her to her waist, her teeth glitter, her eyes, spilling mirth, we know are an intense and brilliant blue. She's no sylph: the boat rocks steeply with her laughter. Large breasts hang low under the sailor blouse. No bra. Her hands, slender and small for so ample a body, grip the oars soundly. Cause of her merriment: a brother overboard. From the bench, the darkly handsome Polish officer looks on. The unlucky brother emerges dripping from the lake and joins him on the bench.

"Who is that girl?" asks the Pole.

The boy shrugs sulkily. He is trying to dry himself with a sodden handkerchief.

"The blonde who laughed at you? Who is she?"

The boy sniffs. "My sister. And you'd better not look at her. We're Jews."

They met once a week for two years in that park. They sat on the same bench. They fed swans. They talked. Held hands. It was always the same: she would never let him walk her home. Someone might see. He was as dark as she was fair, intense as she was gay. On April 1st of the second year, he said to her:

"My friends would make me a laughing stock if they knew I had known a girl two years and never kissed her."

Adela tossed her golden head and turned the hand he held in his so their palms lay close against each other.

"Why do you tell me that?"

His serious dark gaze was now intent upon her. No more moody gazing at the lake. His eyes devoured her.

"Because I'm serious about you, that's why. I am seriously in love with you, that's why."

He wrenched his hand from hers and took her by the shoulders but she only looked away.

"I want to marry you," he said. "On any terms you like."

She closed her eyes and saw her father's head, bent over the prayer book. She closed her eyes and saw her mother's eyes glow as she lit the Sabbath candles. She opened them. Tadeusz's dark and shapely head was bent now over her slender hands. Behind him, the willow buds sprang their faint yellowgreen, like mist. She inclined her head for a moment, and strands of her yellow hair fell forward over the sleek dark head. She tucked them back into the decorous bun she wore.

"Everyone knows what day it is today. April the First."

His head jerked up, eyes full of disbelief.

Clenching her fists until the nails dug in and hurt, she said:

"And you won't make an April Fool of me."

He stood up, bowed and clicked his heels. She never saw Tadeusz again.

"There were girls, you know, even in those days, who had guts. My best friend, Tzimousha, for example. Yes, Moushka showed real guts. She chose the man she married. She collected her 'seven things', I mean all she possessed in the world and she ran away with him. I was a weak, spoiled, pampered girl, the only daughter in a family with four sons and I adored my father. I was almost in love with him. I even married Jacob to please my father. And to help him through a sticky financial patch." She sighed. "It didn't help anyone in the end."

"It never does," said Sarah. "You have to have courage to live for love, but it's the only thing to do."

Adela looked at her daughter-in-law then, as if, for the first time since Jacob died, she knew there was someone else in the room.

"Thank you for coming," she said simply. "I didn't mean to drag you away from work. It was just that – waking up on the floor gave me quite a fright. I didn't know where I was, but I knew it wasn't heaven."

She put the pill box hat in a plastic carrier bag for Sarah. "I could at least have run away," she said. "Girls did that in the olden days. My grandmother Adela, my namesake, was married three times and she ran back home every time. They betrothed them so young, poor little things, and married them off, so they ran away home. I expect I'd have left Jacob a hundred times in that first lonely year of marriage if we'd been in Poland, if I could have gone home and cried and said it was all a mistake and been comforted by my family. But we were in Germany, miles and miles from home and there was my father's pride to consider, and my own pride, too.

"I'd been married just three months when my father came to see how my husband was treating his little girl. That was my chance. Oh, pride! I sat there in my luxurious 'capella' of a flat, surrounded by worldly goods. My father looked so pleased. What a match he'd made! I was sumptuously dressed. I smiled. My husband wasn't beating me. That much was clear. I sat in my ivory tower and – proudly – poured the tea."

5

As soon as you cross the river you can see and feel the difference: South London. In spite of bomb-sites and high-rise flats, playgrounds and factories, it remains the most unchanging part of London since the war. Lambeth. Kennington. Oval. Vauxhall. Fat young women hurry their prams along. Thin elderly men amble. Faces, shop-fronts, hoardings, even dusty privet hedges wear a look of resignation. Sarah smiled to herself, remembering how Adam hated it – hated even to set foot in it: working-class dreariness, he shuddered, lower middle-class respectability, cramped lives. Mel loved it, of course. For her it was timeless, nostalgic, and above all, Socialist. She had to live there.

Sarah marched towards the familiar Victorian terrace, David hop-skipping in front of her like a kangaroo, stopping abruptly now and then so Sarah would bump into him which made him laugh delightedly but tended to make Sarah seasick after the first seventeen times.

Mel seemed comfortable in Lambeth, the pre-first-world-war ambience reminding her of the small northern town where she'd grown up. Sarah and Mel had both imbibed a good deal of Edwardiana in their very different childhoods, some of it from the sayings and the prejudices of adults, most of it from library books.

"Remember the smell?"

"The ones from the school library smelled different from the Public Library ones."

"And the naughty bits in my mother's Boots Library books smelled the best."

"What did they smell of?"

"Oh, bedspreads and . . ."

"Stale 'Shocking'."

"And knickers, of course."

Books passed down by older cousins or aunts might be very 'twenties, but with such an air of "modern" about them they seemed ephemeral and were not to be taken seriously like those solid Edwardian tomes. So the girls shared nostalgia for things they could not possibly remember, and here, in South London, was something of that wonderful E. Nesbit world again: long hot summer afternoons in the Old Kent Road, wide pavements up two steps from the street, a preponderance of pet shops, wares enticingly displayed outside: bird-cages, pups for sale; here was street life: knife sharpeners and menders of cane chairs settled on the kerb for the "duration". Neither of the girls had ever heard a barrel organ, but both thought they had and argued about it.

Passing a young mother pushing a girl-child identical to herself in a push chair, Sarah's beady reporter's eye noted their identical expressions (stolid) and their identical faces (pale and puffy), as she swung through Mel's gate, up the steps, through the house and out into the back yard. David raced off into a corner to join his friends. Sarah sat on the swing and accepted a glass of cold white wine.

"Every morning I have to telephone and check if she's still alive. Then I have to talk her into getting up, and then into living through just one more day. It's hard," said Sarah. Tears fell into her glass, their salt-content spoiling the flavour of the wine. "If only life would return to normal," she sniffed.

Mel snorted. "Normal? What's normal? My dear girl . . . And coming from you . . ."

Mel sat on the steps of a frothy white wrought-iron staircase gazing at the Nigerian twins she held, one in each arm. Sarah thought she looked like someone in a photograph of New Orleans in the bad old days, her large thoroughbred feet bare beneath the uneven hem of a faded cotton dress, her bony wrists bent with the weight of each child. But move the shot a fraction and the backs of Lambeth terrace houses closed in, so that the iron staircase blossomed exotically, an almond tree out of season. Around the two women, children of several races played, laughed and cried. The sound of steel-band music from the council block and the smell of spices confounded the facts: it was tea-time in an English garden. Mel was surely the only registered baby minder in the borough to have read every book on the subject of child care and the new socialism.

"You can snort," said Sarah. "All this death and disaster's Dostoevsky. Not normal life."

"I'm afraid it is," said Mel.

They looked at one another, that level look they could take from no one else.

"What do you expect?" said Mel. "We're getting to the

age. Parents die. Don't kick him!" she yelled across the garden, as wellington boot hove towards golden head. The twins began to cry. She rocked them, and said abruptly: "My father's ill, you know." Sarah didn't. "He isn't getting better. When he dies, my mother will sell the house oop North and move in with me here."

Sarah was appalled. "But you hate your mother."

"I know," said Mel, "and she hates me, too. And we're bad for each other . . . I've never even discussed it with her. I just know that's what we'll do when it comes to it. Here – hold these."

Dumping the twins on Sarah, she strode across the yard, separated two children who were hitting each other with floppy plastic spades, and lifted another off the climbing frame. Returning to Sarah by way of the kitchen, she repossessed the twins, calmly plugged each blackberry mouth with a bottle and sat down on the steps again.

"Mother will have to help me with the children," Mel said. "It will keep her out of mischief."

"If she can curb her racist tongue," said Sarah.

"She'll have to, won't she?" said Mel.

"Darling, *don't*," shrieked Sarah, as David crept up behind her and pushed the swing she sat on. "Now look what you've done. I've spilled all this wine."

Unmoved, David clutched Sarah round her wine-wet knees. "Mummy, may I stay the night? Frankie's staying."

He wiped his palms over his once clean pale-blue shorts and the smell of the best Sancerre rose up fragrantly around them.

"Please."

Sarah questioned Mel with her eyes and caught her exchanging a look with David.

"Conspirators!" she said.

"She said 'yes'," announced David.

Mel nodded. "I confess. I confess. I said yes."

"Then I guess you can."

"Oh, great," David said, and was off again.

The two women sat in the cool of Mel's kitchen, peeling potatoes, shelling peas, drinking Mel's bitter 'tooth-curling' coffee out of mugs.

"Tell me what you say to Adela each morning. What reasons you give her for living."

"Oh, I'm brilliant," said Sarah. "I play all the old standards. Banality's my middle name."

"But what do you say? I mean, she's not religious, is she? She's spent seventy years living other people's lives and now she's lost the man she lived for, so she wants to die. What on earth do you say?"

"Oh, heavy philosophy, I can tell you. Anything to make her get out of bed. Stuff like the smell of coffee or the streaks of sunshine showing up the dust on the kitchen floor. And I say: Adam needs you. *I* need you. Your grandson needs you. She knows it isn't true. She's not stupid. Do you know, in this whole crisis she's never once been stupid, or crass. I admire her very much. Oh, and I go on about doing something, you know, good works, charity for people worse off than she is. I give her cases. It seems every widow thinks she's the only one. Nothing so awful could ever have happened to anyone before. They never talked about one of them dying, you know. Not even the possibility. They made no 'emotional provision', Adam said. Perhaps no one ever believes it will happen to them. I try to persuade her she's good at things and it's worth while doing them. And she is talented. She can paint quite well and do tapestry. But it's an uphill struggle, like pushing a steam-roller up a hill. I'm so tired all the time."

"Well, priests and philosophers don't seem to have come up with much, do they?" said Mel. "Not for someone like Adela. Poor lady, fancy being faced for the first time in your life at seventy years old with questions like why you should get up in the morning if there's no one to get up for."

"And you can't get up for your self."

"You don't know where it is. Or what it is."

Mel went into a passable imitation of a Deep South accent: "Now, where did ah put ma self? I guess I put it on some shelf. . ." She made two knives tap dance on the table, then, reverting to her normal voice, she said, "I suppose the only person Adela loves enough to live for now is Adam, and he's not going to let her live for him, or through him, is he? The burden would be too great."

"She's going to have to live for him – at a distance."

"You dare not allow it. She's got to learn to live for its own sake, and for herself."

"But that's the problem. We've just been through that. How do you get someone who has never lived their own life to start now, at seventy years of age?"

Sarah banged her mug down on the chopping board.

"Can you give someone a life, a purpose, an identity, so late in the day? People think I'm trying to put her back on her own two feet again, but she's never stood on them before. It's an identity crisis I'm dealing with. Who is she now that she's no longer Mrs Jacob Cornish?"

"You're much more desperate, aren't you, about getting

Adela off your back and onto her own feet than you were when your own father died and your mother was first widowed."

Sarah said slowly: "I suppose I am."

"You're as shocked by this death as if you've never experienced death before. Yet your own father died."

"Yes. Isn't it strange?"

"Perhaps it isn't strange," said Mel. "You're doing this for Adam. You're desperate on his behalf. Having a widowed Mum around could ruin *his* life. Worse, it could ruin the sacred career. And that would hit you where you live."

"You mean I live that much through Adam? *Still?* Maybe it's true. If I feel his father's death more keenly than my own, it must be true. I was close to my father while I was growing up. I suppose I defend myself instinctively – we all do – against direct blows. When the blow is aimed at Adam I don't defend myself."

"You defend him. You interpose your body."

"I steel myself to take it straight on the nose. I'm taking it for him."

"So the first impact doesn't reach him. Do people realize when they buy a Mark-Sarah wife they're getting full protection from all life's blows? We may be the first lot of women who've tried to do everything ourselves, without servants: be wives, mothers, mistresses, pals, colleagues, housekeepers, headcooks and bottlewashers, but honestly, Sarah, this is ridiculous."

"I know."

Sarah's voice, which had dropped to a whisper, stopped altogether and for a few moments there was silence in the kitchen, except for the noise of the children from the garden and the ticking of a clock. Their fingers paused among unpeeled potatoes and unshelled peas and each knew that there was fear on the rapt face of the other. As if by pact, each of them kept their gaze on their own hands, and the objects in their hands, until the moment passed.

"It's as if we've all lived our lives underground," Sarah said softly. "In a tunnel. Never coming up for air. The women of the past lived only through others, vicariously. It's what we must learn not to do. They had no options. They accepted the rôles: first you were a daughter, then a wife, then a mother. You, yourself were hidden by your label. People might never know your name." She took a swig of the cold and bitter coffee. "Would you believe I'm still doing it?" she said.

"Then you had used it all up," Mel said. "The time, I mean." She emptied the peeled potatoes into a saucepan and put them on to boil. "Finish, good lady, the bright day is done, and we are for the dark." Outside in the yard, a baby howled. Brandishing a colander in one hand, she clattered down the iron staircase, declaiming. Mel to the rescue! "Unarm, Eros, the long day's task is done, and we must sleep."

Reappearing with a sodden bundle, she demanded of Sarah: "Do you notice the difference? The woman talks about darkness and light, the man about work. Life is just one long task for men, isn't it, little one?" she crooned, unpinning a rankly smelling disposable nappy and dropping it into the rubbish bin on top of the potato peelings.

"Is that a male or female child?" asked Sarah nastily.

Mel held the baby expertly, while she smeared baby lotion round a delicate bud-like penis.

"See for yourself. His name is Nathaniel. He's four months old."

"How do you do?" said Sarah. "Hey, listen, I must get home, I have to help Adam pack. He's off to Africa again tomorrow to film the emergence of yet another state."

"They don't emerge, these days, till the TV cameras are set up, I've noticed. Is that the head I see emerging, doctor? Black mothers are so hopelessly uncontrolled. Just hold it, will you, while we frame this shot."

"I think it's true that men change when they lose their fathers. I've noticed it with Adam. He has more authority, these days, at work, and at home, too, with David. As if, now he feels he can play the father."

"Yet we've been playing mothers all our lives," said Mel.

6

ENCOUNTERS/ENCOUNTERS

Anyone she met who might be useful, interesting or amusing was summoned to her ancient mansion flat above the Cromwell Road. It might be the worst day of the week for you, the most inconvenient time, the most inclement weather. The Cromwell Road might be impossible to reach from where you were. No matter. This was no invitation. It was a command.

"Daarling," growled the dark brown, almost masculine voice on the telephone, the voice of a large, dominating, neutered cat, perhaps. A cat with presence. "You haven't been to *see* me." Pause while the reproach sunk in and guilt took a good hold. Then – snap! "Come tomorrow. Four o'clock." Click. She'd rung off. You got no time to remonstrate. Orders were orders. Of course, if you were that determined, you could ring back and say no. People seldom said no to Moura.

You battered through tube train crowds to Earls Court station or sat tight in a taxi in a permanent traffic jam by the Science Museum. And when you arrived, the portals of the old mansion block spelled gloom and names with more handles to them than the creaky ancient lift. You rang the bell and heard it clanging, the unsmiling Italian maidservant smelling of stuffy *pensiones* and rectitude opened the door as formally as ever. "Please to wait here. The Baroness will not be long."

The ante rooms of a winter palace. St. Petersburg, 1909. The year Count Zakrevski's lively young daughter was presented to Society. The year Moura was seventeen and "came out".

Pictures, prints, old maps of the streets of Moscow. An ikon or two. Rugs, tapestries, embroidered cushions. An onyx egg in an ornate box, the word "Fabergé" written in Cyrillic on it, a small framed photo of Moura at seventeen. No amount of Fabergé or fustian can obscure the eagerness in that round, pretty, unrecognizable face. Could that kitten have become this cat?

Tap, tap, she leans on a walking stick to cross the parquet floor, her square jaw set, her cheeks a little flushed: they've opened her hip again, but we don't mention it. This is a lady who has said "fuck off" to Death. He did, of course. It is difficult not to obey the Baroness. She was lying in bed in her hairnet with only an old nightdress on when she saw him. The Uninvited. He dared to come into this room where samplers, photos, pills and relics and above all piles of books protected her. She looked him in the eye. "I'll send for *you* when I want you. Fuck off, Death."

"Daarling!" She kisses me. Her cheek is smooth, well-rouged. She smells of good face powder and cologne. Her dark grey hair's been given a bluish rinse and is nicely done, with a small net veil which covers her forehead, too. She's carefully dressed, as always. Her jewellery matches. She sends the maid for some vodka and admires my ring.

"My husband brought it for me from Mexico."

It's a silver fish which curls round my finger beautifully. Moura tries it on. "I'm Pisces, you know." She swigs her little glass of vodka in one swallow, watching me as I take my gingerly sips. Her laugh is a low purring sound which ends in a giggle. It is four o'clock and she knows that I long for a cup of tea.

"I know your birthday, Moura, and I know your sign." What a party her eightieth had been: flowers, tributes, presents, endless distinguished guests. I hold out my hand to her. "May I have my ring?"

Moura pours another vodka and hands me the silver fish. "Next time he goes to Mexico ask him to bring *me* one," she growls. "It *is* my sign." She sighs, leans back. Tries to assess my mood. "I was very impressed with your husband. *Most* impressed. And I don't say that about young men nowadays."

"Thank you," I manage faintly, noting that Moura's attempts to charm fail nowadays. That what pervades the room is strength rather than grace, force and indomitable will. She's got nerve, Moura, and this is what one likes in her. That and her gravelly, no nonsense, wit.

The snapshot we've used of Moura with H. G. Wells and Gorky catches something of her spirit. An impish smile. An alert and vital look. I doubt if Moura was ever a beauty, but her feline fascination captivated some remarkable men.

Her first marriage, at nineteen, was to an Estonian, Count von Benckendorff, who courted her in England while she was at Cambridge and he was at the Russian Embassy in London. They had four children, and lived the privileged life of Russian aristocrats before the Revolution. Moura's style is still essentially aristocratic. She holds court now in the Cromwell Road, where courtiers are admitted at half hourly intervals throughout the day. And the strangest cross-section they are, but that's traditional. There is the story Janet Flanner tells of going round Washington in a taxi with Moura. "Oh, it's just like our old country house in the Ukraine!" exclaimed Moura, when she saw the White House.

In Year One of the Revolution she lost her husband, her father, her fortune and her way of life. She crossed Estonia on foot, she rescued her children by smuggling them through to the Baltic estate where they were guarded by the English governess who had been her teacher, she went to jail, she escaped, she fell in love. And then she went to jail again.

Violent times beget violent passions, and what we have here is that rare but genuine article, A REVOLUTIONARY ROMANCE. Our romantic hero – Robert Bruce Lockhart, the dashing young British diplomat. Our heroine, young, lovely, fiery and dispossessed? None other than the Countess Moura von Benckendorff. Fade in, St Petersburg in the hush of the first days of the revolution. March 1918. It is Moura's twenty-sixth birthday. The treaty of Brest-Litovsk is signed. Trotsky is appointed President of the new Bolshevik Supreme War Council. St Petersburg is evacuated by the government. Trotsky promises Bruce Lockhart that he will be personally responsible for housing the British Mission safely in Moscow. The price? Company. If Bruce Lockhart will agree to remain in St Petersburg for another week, he and Trotsky can travel to Moscow together.

"It was a memorable week," he wrote later in his *Memoirs of a British Agent*. He met Moura and it changed his life.

"A Russian of the Russians, she had a lofty disregard for all the pettiness of life," he wrote, "and a courage which was proof against all cowardice. Her vitality, due perhaps to an iron constitution, was immense, and invigorated everyone with whom she came into contact. Where she loved, there was her world, and her philosophy of life had made her mistress of all the consequences. She was an aristocrat. She could have been a communist. She could never have been a bourgeoise."

I have seen Moura roar with laughter at this description, yet every detail of her presence was impressed upon Bruce Lockhart's heart.

"She arrived [to stay at the British Mission in Moscow] at ten o'clock in the morning, and I was engaged with interviews until ten minutes to one. I went downstairs to the living room where we had our meals. She was standing by a table, and the spring sun was shining on her hair. As I walked forward to meet her, I scarcely dared to trust my voice. Into my life something had entered which was stronger than any other tie, stronger than life itself."

It was clear, even to a British diplomat half in love with Russia and her Revolution, that freedom was not long to be breathed in Russian air. An atmosphere of suspense which heightened all emotions hung over Moscow, making everything – the words of gypsy songs, the deep notes of Russian voices, the warm stillness of summer nights and the fragrance of lime trees – seem haunting and unforgettable.

On the day of young Dora Kaplan's notorious attempt on Lenin's life, Moura and Bruce Lockhart drove out to the Sparrow Hills together to watch the sun rise over the Kremlin. "It came up like an angry ball of fire heralding destruction. No joy was to come with the morning." That night they were both arrested and put in prison. The reign of the Red Terror had begun.

Moura soon got herself released and set about the rescue of her friend. First, she sent him a basket "with clothes, books, tobacco, coffee, ham, a long letter and a pack of cards". With these he played terrifying games of Chinese patience with himself, gambling his life daily against the cards: if he could not get the patience out, he would not get out of the Kremlin alive. Next, she came to visit him with no less a personage than Jacob Peters, one of the Chieftains of the Terror.

"This was the most thrilling moment of

my captivity," he wrote. Peters was in a talkative mood, but Lockhart listened only fitfully. He was watching Moura, who was standing behind Peters and was "fiddling with my books, which stood on a small side table surmounted by a long hanging mirror. She caught my eyes, held up a note, and slipped it into a book. I was terrified. A slight turn of his head, and Peters could see everything in the mirror. I gave the tiniest of nods. Moura, however, seemed to think I had not seen, and repeated the performance. My heart stopped beating, and this time I nodded like an epileptic. Fortunately, Peters noticed nothing, or Moura's shrift would have been short... As soon as they had gone I rushed to the book – it was Carlyle's *French Revolution* – and took out the note. It was very short. Six words only: SAY NOTHING. ALL WILL BE WELL. That night I could not sleep."

A week later Lockhart was free.

Moura spent every second of his last two days in Russia with him in the Kremlin, helping him to pack his belongings, his books, the pack of patience cards, the letters she had sent him on Cheka notepaper. Talking and smoking incessantly. Helping him sort out the confusion in his mind. She knew he was strongly tempted to stay with her in Russia but she did not encourage him. Russian fatalism? Perhaps. "I had been the centre of a miniature world storm," he wrote, "and I knew that my official obligation was to return." Months before Moura had described Bruce Lockhart to himself: "A little clever but not clever enough, a little strong but not strong enough, a little weak but not weak enough." Does that sound like the man Moura would want always at her side?

"The train was drawn up at a siding . . . In the cool starlit night Moura and I discussed trivialities. We talked of everything but ourselves. And then I made her go home. I watched her go until she had disappeared into the night. Then I turned into my dimly lit carriage to wait and to be alone with my thoughts . . ."

In August 1924 Moura and Robert Bruce Lockhart met in Vienna for the first time since they had parted on that starlit station in 1918. They walked in the Vienna Woods and talked. "She told me all about her life, her imprisonment, her escapes,, her meeting with Gorky. She looks older. Her face is more serious and she has a few grey hairs. She was not dressed as in the old days, but she had not changed. The change is in me. I admire her above all other women. Her mind, her genius, her control are all wonderful. But the old feeling has gone."

Many men loved Moura, but whom did Moura love? Language – always so important to her – may be a clue. Moura speaks several languages fluently, but none so lovingly as she speaks Italian. The famous Russian writer Maxim Gorky lived in Sorrento. Moura lived and worked there with him over a period of seventeen years.

"I worked in the next room, dictating, translating, talking." A low chuckle. "He got accustomed to my voice. He used to say 'I like to hear the sound of you in the next door room.'" She purrs with private amusement as she recollects their intimacy. What images recur from those days of work, wine, roses and revolutions? Suddenly she snorts, snuffles and shakes with merriment. "Gorky was proud of his legs," she tells me. "He used to admire them in the mirror while he was getting dressed, turning this way and that, showing them off to me. 'Say what you like,' he used to say, 'I've got legs like a Cossack'." She guffaws. It is a full-throated, Russian, quite unfeminine guffaw, and entirely characteristic.

The great Gorky apparently had a great love for animals, especially dogs. Robert Bruce Lockhart reported it to his diary. "At Sorrento he had a pedigree fox terrier bitch called Piksha (the name of a coarse Russian fish) and a mongrel whippet. In 1919 in Russia when H. G. Wells was staying with him he had a Great Dane. It went everywhere with Gorky. It was called Diane. It even went for walks with Wells. One day it went for a walk by itself and never came back. It had been eaten by a starving populace. During the late twenties and early thirties, Gorky started going back to Russia on visits, and after 1933 he was persuaded to stay there. He died in '36. It is probable that he was murdered, and that the instrument was poison. He was eaten by the ever hungry Terror, and like the dog that went for a walk by itself, he, too, never came back."

I waited for Moura in an Italian trattoria she liked because it reminded her of her days in Sorrento with Gorky. It was small and dark and cool and I started on the Campari. After ten minutes I was eyeing the antipasto trolley hungrily. After fifteen minutes another Campari was due. By twenty past one I was worried. Moura was not usually late. At half past one, a small commotion could be heard at the door, the tapping of a stick, obeisances made. Flushed and undaunted she ordered food and wine in her perfect Italian and we made two toasts. One because the taxi she was in had had an accident. Everyone involved had been shaken or hurt or detained in hospital: the driver of the cab, the driver of the other car, and two passengers. Moura had been late. For which she apologized.

The second toast (we'd reached the second bottle) was to health. She'd been that morning to the hospital and they'd checked her out. Her heart was sound. Blood pressure fine. She told me this shyly and I felt honoured with the information. She was girlishly happy. We giggled and drank and lapsed into indiscretion.

"I want to ask you something, Moura. Have you ever had more than one lover at a time?"

"What? No, I don't think so. Let me think. There was a time once in Moscow when they overlapped . . ."

I leaned forward eagerly. Now might I learn something from the grand "mistress of all the consequences".

"I *hated* it," said Moura emphatically. "It was only a few weeks, but such a strain."

I laughed immoderately.

With H. G. Wells her life had taken on the hectic social pattern she keeps up to this day. They went everywhere: film shows, previews, meetings, first nights, parties, talks. They played cards into the small hours at his house in Hanover Terrace, Regent's Park. "As pronounced by Moura," commented a disapproving Lockhart to his diary, "it sounds like Hangover Terrace," adding sourly: "H. G. had five front teeth out – nothing wrong with them – he's just afraid they won't last as long as he intends to live." Moura found some of their score cards the other day and showed them to me: H. G. had covered them in his fluent hand, adding little drawings and jokes and limericks about winning and losing. The rows of figures under each initial are heroic: they must have played for nights on end and lost empires. "Except for his women, Wells has no real men friends," notes Lockhart.

They must have made a disconcerting couple. Moura loved arguing politics with Wells, especially Russian and foreign politics, and preferably in public. She could dominate any conversation and frequently did so, rendering Wells somewhat "crotchety" at times. Lockhart records a luncheon at Boulestin where she gave Randolph Churchill some "good cracks", then left for Paris, accompanied (to the station only) by H. G. Once, H. G. was lunching at the Berkeley Grill with a rather "sexy" American girl. And who should be discovered at the very next table but Moura, lunching with the diarist himself. The four apparently joined up for coffee but the wretched diarist did not, for once, record the dialogue. Such an astonishing silence, however, must indicate the force of it, don't you think?

I knew Moura only at the end of her life and she had that disturbing androgynous quality old women acquire. It is not simply the flattened breasts or the tendency to sit with their knees apart, nor the determination they no longer bother to hide. And it's not the hair which grows on their faces, nor their developing jowls. In Moura's case, her face had become very square and her jaw prominent. All her strength seemed to reside, those last few years, in that jaw. For all her feline qualities, there was something of the bulldog, something Churchillian about her. "I'll fight on the hills and I'll fight on the beaches," said that thrust-out jaw of hers. "They'll never defeat me." And this bulldog determination sat uneasily with the careful cat-like arrangement of hair under its little sparkler-studded net kept on with tiny bows, the rouged and powdered cheeks, the trail of scent.

It was leaving her winter palace in the Cromwell Road which broke her, finally. It was the sound of the axes in the cherry trees. She stood, tearful and displaced among the débris of her life, books piled in dusty heaps, crates stacked with memories, ancient trunks stuck with the faded labels of happier times.

"I don't want to leave," she told me. "I don't know really, why I'm going. It's a combination of things: the rent going up, the feeling in the family that now I'm getting old I should live near my son in Tuscany." She looked at me with a flash of the old glint, the old disdain. "I think Tuscany is a good place to die, don't you? Under those clear blue skies." Her look dared me to disagree.

"It's a rotten place to die, Moura. Everywhere is a rotten place to die."

But Moura had made up her mind. She

would decide her own fate as usual, and the Horseman had been informed.

"You will come and see me in Italy," she commanded, and I said of course I would.

The traffic thundered its usual dull fury as I waited to cross the Cromwell Road, and I knew then that He who had been Banished would come for her under those Tuscan skies. I would never see Moura again.

7

Adam was packing to go back to Africa again. A pile of carefully folded underwear lay in one case. Desert boots, canvas shoes, sandals, lined another. He held up a sweater for Sarah's inspection.

"Do you think I'll need this?"

She shook her head, and took the sweater from him, folding it neatly into a drawer. He held up a jacket. "I'm fond of this."

"Too heavy," said Sarah. "You are fond of lots of things you have to leave behind."

Adam raised half an eyebrow. "You could get it cleaned for me while I'm away."

"Okay. Cleaning pile over here."

"Now, let's see . . ." he pursed his lips and surveyed the scene. "Pyjamas, socks, short sleeved shirts. Brush. Comb. Toothpaste. Remember the time I left my hairbrush behind and you had to send it to me in Peru?"

"With six jars of coffee and a crate of your favourite loo paper. You could have bought every one of those things on the spot."

"What, in the high Andes?" said Adam indignantly. "They'd have been different brands."

"Well don't sit on your glasses in the plane this time."

"Or drop them at the bottom of the Embassy swimming pool."

"The best was the time you left your passport on the breakfast table, and it zoomed up, in close-shot, and hit me in the face."

"And you paged the airport in seven languages."

"And sat on the edge of a taxi seat with it all the way to Heathrow. But I caught you."

Adam looked at her, and there was something shy in the look, though they'd known one another for ever.

"You always do," he said.

Sarah and David stood at the window, as usual, watching and waving. Adam's hand, a pale pennant stuck through the open window, waving, was the last they saw of him as the car went round the familiar bend. What if it really were the last? Like wives everywhere, Sarah allowed herself a moment of fear in which a plane crashed, a jeep skidded, a snake bit. Then she closed her mind firmly against such thoughts and struggled to re-open panels marked "Reason" and "Control".

"Will I never get used to it?" she asked herself, "no matter how often he goes away?"

The first leaves on her beloved plane trees had begun to fall. Gold against green, they lay, a bright pattern on the grass below. It would soon be autumn. She turned from the window.

"Come on, Mummy," said David. "I'll be late for school."

Through the plate glass doors of her office she went, past the potted palms and into the lift. A tall, slim figure in a soft white suit with a white cashmere knotted over it was the only other occupant and he leaned back wearily against the shiny lift interior, hat tilted forward to shade exhausted eyes.

"Robert!" she said.

The character surveyed her through the smoke of his Gauloise and the fumes of his after shave. A smile like the cat that's licked up a month's supply of cream suffused his face.

"I'm pooped," he announced happily. "Shagged out. Fucked silly. I might even have fucked it off!"

"These art directors! Boy, girl, or some of each?"

"Oooh, cheeky," he whistled. "I'm into girls right now – " He leaned over and pinched her breast. "I thought you'd be on to that."

He sighed and leaned back again as if he could not stand.

"If you want to know I've just been sprung from a suite at the Savoy, where a lion lady fashion editress from another town has had me locked up all weekend. I was supposed to photograph her for this feature, you see. On Friday night. And when I went in, she'd got all her clothes out on the bed so I could choose what she would wear for the shot. Well, I made her try them all on. She's in her fifties, this doll, and she's terrific. I only hope I look as good twenty years from now. And I made her take them all off. And then I tried them on. And then I took them off. Then we locked the door. And then we rang for room service."

"So you had to unlock the door."

They passed together down the corridor, dimly aware of

the giggles of minions, of Adrian's raised eyebrow and Geoffrey's cold stare. They swept into the Art Department and closed the door.

"Now this," Robert said, producing a blow up of a marvellous face, full of character and memories, "is your protrait of Naomi . . ."

"Mitchison." Sarah peered. "Well, yes. It's true I described her as a female Auden, face like a map . . ."

"Dear *girl*," Robert said, patiently, "I *know* what you wrote. I'm not one of the morons who run this place. I'm me."

"It's wonderful, Robert."

A grunt.

"There's a chance, just a chance, mind, I may get permission to use this one, too." He held up an elderly snapshot for her to see.

"Oh, fantastic! It's her in the get-up she wore as the Spring Queen. How she shocked them at all those parties!"

"I'm not surprised. Just a few sheaves of this and that unstrategically placed. Pretty daring."

"And so was her book, *The Corn King and the Spring Queen*. Bloomsbury used it as a sex manual."

"So that's what was wrong with them," said Robert with satisfaction. "I always wondered. Now, this. For Steiglitz's lady in her New York 1940 period house. Is this what you had in mind?"

"It's perfect," she breathed. He had made a collage: Steiglitz's famous New York sidewalk scenes, some cover designs from the arts magazine they'd edited together, Steiglitz's camera and a painter's brush, and had superimposed upon it the face of the subject when rich, young and beautiful. Dorothy Norman, this is your life! "The only thing missing is that 1940's house, so perfect in every detail. She still lives in it, so it is important . . ."

"You can't have everything. Will you never learn that?"

"I hope not," said Sarah.

"And Laura?"

They peered into the light box at a strangely foreshortened picture of a woman standing alone in the centre of an empty room, empty except for a wicker cradle.

"I hate that distortion, that lens . . ."

"But it's right, don't you see? Isn't she the professor's wife who went gay when he left her and fixed for her lover to have a baby so she could be its mother? Then the girl who had the baby fell in love with someone else, and took the baby away. You look at that picture. It's exactly right."

She looked. "You want to be careful of Daphne," she warned. "She's into astrology of the higher kind, and she thinks she's a witch. She'll fix us if she hates it." A pause. "You're wonderful, Robert."

"They all say that," he said, mollified. He leaned across the light box and kissed her lightly on the lips. "You only say it because it's true."

He switched off the light box with a flourish. The swish of the curtain. Sarah laughed. "Now that you've turned the lights down low I'm beginning to see the light."

Arm in arm, they did a neat soft shoe shuffle to the door.

She went into her office and rang her mother.

"Still the same problem," said Dolly. "I wake up at four o'clock and I want to go back to sleep more than anything and I can't. And I can't read anymore. I can't concentrate. I used to be such a reader. You remember, Sarah. This morning I got up at five and took my breakfast back to bed, and listened to the pig prices on the early morning programme for farmers. Then I had my bath and it was still only half past six. I was baking by seven o'clock. I made the biscuits you like, Sarah, because they're difficult, you have to grind the nuts, which takes a bit of time. Then I made some soup, my special carrot one. You know. Yes, of course you can have the recipe. Here it is. One pound of carrots, one pint of water, a large onion, chopped. Glaze it in butter, stew it gently with the carrots, stir in the stock when the carrots are soft, add seasoning and sugar, just a pinch – it brings out the flavour of the carrots, bring to the boil, then simmer for an hour with the lid tight on. Cool and then blend. I stir in cream to serve and add chopped parsley as a garnish. You can add croutons done in butter if you like. Both those are optional of course. Well, I made that soup this morning, after I'd baked the biscuits, then I went for a walk, and by the time I came back it was eleven. It's as if something drives me, drives me, all the time. What have you been doing?" she asked unexpectedly.

"Oh, I'm busy. Very busy. Doing the sort of things you used to do. Living other people's lives."

"Yes. I was always busy in those days."

"Doing everything except getting down to myself," said Sarah. "I'm a long way down."

"As long as you've always got someone to do things for," Sarah's mother said sadly. "That's the trick."

If that's the trick, then loser takes all, thought Sarah.

Next, she rang Adela who was on to a new tack called "Do you think we did everything we could?" This involved going over every word every doctor or ward sister or nurse had said, combing them for contradictions, and ending up certain that if he had taken this advice instead of that, this medicine instead of that, had this operation instead of that, the patient would not have died.

"In the end, it's God's Will," said Sarah, desperately.

"I know. But God's Will could have been done in five or ten years' time."

To divert Adela from this, Sarah asked: "And what were you doing when I telephoned?"

Adela giggled. "Well, it's a funny thing," she said, "You know how I always hated opera and how Daddy loved it? You know how I never went with him – well hardly ever – and he had to go and sit there by himself? Well, now I seem to want to do everything he liked to do. And when there's an opera on, I have to watch, or listen to it, for him. I wait for all the arias and nod to them in just the way he did, and talk to him about it – you know, 'she wasn't so good on the high notes', that sort of thing, or 'Victoria de Los Angeles did it better'. I can't understand it, Sarah. Perhaps I'm becoming him."

"It seems to be something widows do when they're recently bereaved," Sarah said. "I remember my mother doing something of the kind. She always hated Daddy's interest in newspapers and the television news. She used to tease him about it all the time. And after he died she would listen religiously to every news broadcast and read the papers column by column inch herself, just as he had done. I suppose it makes you feel that the person's still there."

Adrian was cutting out photographs of film stars, like a

child who's been given a scrapbook for Christmas.

"I'd like to talk to you," she said.

"Talk," Adrian told her, passing her a picture of Vivien Leigh in *The Mask of Virtue* and sighing deeply. "Wasn't she beautiful? Wouldn't you die to look like that?"

"I've been thinking," said Sarah.

Adrian assumed a basso profundo voice, "A dangerous habit in gels," he growled.

"I'd like to do another series sometime," she told him. "About women who became their husbands. I've researched it a bit, and it's quite a phenomenon. There are the widows who know every word or note or line of their husbands' work by heart and who spend their lives promoting him, and there are . . ." she became aware that Adrian had paused in his work and was staring at her.

"What about husbands who 'become' their wives?" he said.

Oh God, I've done it now, Sarah thought. He knows I'm on to him and Adriana. But Adrian collected himself and said sharply.

"If I were any of the other editors of this journal, I'd say that next time you should do extraordinary old men; because I'm me, I know you shouldn't. It wouldn't be half as interesting. It couldn't be. Whoever heard of 'fast' gentlemen?"

"Women are still performing dogs," Sarah said. "Anything they do that is at all out of the ordinary – even living their lives to the full – is considered rare, like dogs standing on their hind legs. They are not expected to achieve. People still ask women at parties if they 'do' anything."

Adrian put his hand on her shoulder. "Sarah, you know what I always say. If I had your brothers in my department instead of you bright gels, the level of intelligence would drop by twenty per cent overnight."

For the first time the sadness of his situation struck her more forcibly than the comedy or the threat of it: here was a man with an impressive male physique, who admired women so much he had wanted desperately all his life to be one. Preferably an impeccably lesbian turn-of-the-century French bluestocking. Dignity prevented him from changing his body; he could only clothe it in female apparel and present it as female wherever the circumstances allowed. And the circumstances were rare. She had a sudden glimpse into his past: a boy child besotted with his mother, a busy young person much given to charitable work, always dashing out and leaving the small boy staring forlornly through the window at her departing carriage. What does he do when she's gone? He wanders into her room, inhales the female smell of it, the unmade bed, the pile of discarded undies. He sniffs them. He puts them on. He stares in the mirror. If he screws up his eyes, he resembles his mother. He is said to be just like her. Everyone remarks upon it. His hair is still long and in curls. He gathers it up inexpertly and fixes it with a comb. He bites his lips and pinches his cheeks as he has seen her do. He looks again. And this time, unscrews his eyes. He *is* his mother. An extraordinary feeling of belonging to the world envelopes him. As long as that image is in the mirror, he feels safe. For a few moments in the child's daily round of disciplines and disappointments, he is – simply – happy.

Sarah thought suddenly of the question Adrian asked every new girl who joined his department on the first day of "term". She had always been puzzled by it.

"Who would you most like to be, if you could choose to be

anyone at all in the whole wide world?" he'd ask gleefully, his eyes round with excitement as he waited for the answer. How Sarah had disappointed him! Of course she'd longed to *look* like Vivien Leigh. Didn't every woman? But the idea of *being* someone else had never occurred to her. She had presumed that you were stuck with yourself for life and had to struggle to become, to fully realize that self before dying.

A jolly, fat girl from the Beauty department rushed in, closed the door and collapsed, giggling, into a chair.

"You're never going to believe what's going on," she said. "Every male on the staff is in such a state . . . I think they'll explode if it goes on like this. The tension's been building for about a week. Have you tried to talk to any of them? Or get any work done?" She started to hiccup and Adrian got her some water, then patiently patted her back.

"Come on then, dear. Spit it out."

It had started a week ago, when Mary Jane who gave the advice on the problem page was asked by a reader if the reader's husband's whatsit, which the reader had measured, it seemed, was bigger or smaller than usual. With her customary cool, Mary Jane had replied that much research had been done on the subject, though not by Mary Jane, and it seemed a consensus had been reached: six inches was the average length of the average extended male whatsit.

"Since then," the girl from the Beauty department reported, "there hasn't been a ruler to be seen on the premises, let alone a tape measure. The men were looking daggers at one another all the time, if that was the word, and it was whispered that one of them had established a mirror behind one of the loos in the men's executive washroom and a similar mirror behind his loo at home. Mary Jane had been threatened with the sack and the editor had been threatened with divorce and had been heard to mutter darkly about the company retired matrons of respectable teaching hospitals, (for such was Mary Jane) must keep.

Coming down, the lift was full of secretaries and scooter-messenger boys with crash helmets and alarming rocker regalia, all gleaming black leather and studs, poised for the death defying speed which was of course necessary to transport one negative, one page, one prop, one memo, from one part of London to another.

"Have you done it yet with earphones on?" grinned one teenager to another. "It's a gas. Terrific. It's the latest thing."

"Yeah. You should get a head set. Only way to fly."

"But you can't share them. I mean you can't put one earphone of the same set on each person's ear, can you? Wouldn't stretch."

"Nah. You gotta have one set each. It's inside your head. It's great."

"Don't you get outa sync?"

"Nah. You're each doing it to your own music."

As Sarah went out through the front door of the building she met Geoff, who was coming in. He looked at her. Then he stopped. Then he ostentatiously shot his cuff and looked at his watch. Then he looked at her again.

Sarah tossed her head and walked on. But it rankled. How it rankled! God, it made her angry, the whole damn stupid attitude. She didn't have a desk job. How did he think she got all those interviews if she never went out in the afternoon? Didn't think, any of them, that was the point. Well, she was damned if she'd justify herself to them. She got results, didn't she? Let them fault her on her results. It wasn't good enough, she knew that. They were there, you see, all of them, from nine to five, with an hour, more or less, for lunch. They did little in that time, they produced less, but they were there in the office, ergo: they worked. Sarah was out of the office more than she was in it. She came in just as others were leaving. She went out when they were coming in. Was that *work?* Women! They just didn't understand the rules. To men, office life was sacred, the work place a hallowed place. Human emotions, family responsibilities, the ghastly grown-up rôles one had to play at home, were all shucked off when one reached the ordered safety of one's office. Nothing could touch one here. A man was free to concentrate on higher things. Like work. One might have to manufacture a little of the stuff occasionally, so that one's secretary would have something more to do. But the rules got one through: one could hold a meeting to decide to hold a meeting which might decide that a two-day conference was needed. And then there were the minutes of the meeting, and the memos re the minutes, and the filing of the memos and the minutes of the meeting. And the wall charts giving dates and venues of the meetings for the next five years, with red and blue pins stuck in them and flags and sliding sections in case of change. You could play with those for hours.

By the time Sarah had done her interview and got to Mel's she was fuming.

"There's steam coming out of your ears," said Mel. "Calm down." She poured them both large Scotches and sat on the floor in her old blue jeans, an apple resting snugly in her crotch. The New Eve.

"Two people making love to different music at the same time," Mel said reflectively, turning a Debussy record to the other side. "That puts the tin lid on it. Why bother? Are you communicating? Are you in touch? Are you together in any sense at all?"

She rummaged amongst last Sunday's newspapers. "Both Barbara Castle and Shirley Williams would agree with you about men at work," she said. "You should hear what they have to say about the House of Commons. Aha, I've found it. I want to read you what Shirley Williams says about femininity. She says it is 'most of all not being bound by unnecessary rules. The House of Commons,' she says 'is a marvellous example of an almost totally male institution. It's absolutely riddled by rules that it has made for itself. Most of them are quite unnecessary, like those in a boys' school. And femininity is asking yourself all the time what human purpose is being served'."

Sarah wandered through the silent flat. The student au pair was at a disco. David was fast asleep, one hand clutching his "roonya", his baby word for the famous striped flannel, the other holding a toy globe of the world. She leaned over and gently took the globe from him, putting it carefully on a crowded shelf above the bed. She watched as he flung himself over in his sleep, uncovering himself. Tonight he had wanted stories about Africa. She would have to brush up on Africa. She covered him thoughtfully. She hadn't been too brilliant on the subject tonight, she knew.

She went into the bedroom and saw Adam's suits hanging there where she had left them that morning, waiting to be cleaned and pressed. She took them by the hangers and put them in the hall ready for tomorrow. As she moved them a familiar smell rose up: his smell. She hung them by the door and smoothed their sleeves, the beige, the blue, the brown velvet corduroy. She thought of the smell he brought back with him so often from his travels, the smell of nights spent on planes, that peculiar scent of pressurization. She wondered where he was, and if he would phone her soon. She thought of Adela and the astrakhan hat. No wonder the poor old thing had fainted when the whole contraption swung towards her. She thought of Dolly in her empty house, no child sleeping, no job, or loving telephone call awaiting.

She went to her favourite window overlooking the square. It was wide open to the fading summer light and to the small breeze coming up on the night air. Some petals from her pink geraniums caught the breeze and were detached by it, floating down slowly past other windows to lie unheeded on the paving stones.

Her downstairs neighbour's daughter was learning the guitar and writing her own songs. She caught the drift, plaintive, if thin.

Outside my window
Flowers glow
Their petals blow
Away

Who can say why
The leaves will fall
The summer fade
Away

Only I wait
Inanimate.

Lights began to go on across the square. People laughed, squabbled, got into cars, slammed doors, went off for the evening. Sarah remembered suddenly how excluded they'd often felt, she and Adam, when they were very young. There was always a party somewhere but it wasn't here.

Eventually, even the randiest pigeons were quiet. A girl came to a window opposite and began, methodically, to brush her hair.

We try so hard to be whole, to be strong, to be independent, Sarah thought. All over the world each evening women make the same gestures: putting children to bed, tidying the house, preparing food, applying lipstick, brushing our hair. And trying, while doing all these things. Always trying. To find out who we are, what we are. And at the end of it all, is this all we are, we women without men? Just a bunch of women, waiting?

8

Poland 1924. A covered verandah full of potted plants, geraniums, palms. Adela plays cards there with her grandmother who is also called Adela. The old woman is winning, as usual, cunning old thing. Despite her great age (she lived to be over a hundred), despite an ear trumpet and a set of false teeth which could be heard in the next village, despite three marriages and a somewhat louche career as favourite pawnbroker to whole regiments of dashing young Austro-Hungarian Army officers, despite all this and the long ago loss of the delicate dark beauty she had been renowned for – or perhaps because of it – the old woman always won at cards. "Piatrick's grandchild!" she crowed, at the end of every game, the name we had for the winner, don't ask me why, and her wicked old eye would gleam: she knew just what her winnings were! Oh, she was *rafineer!*

One of my friends rushed in from next door in a state of excitement: "Adelaida, your father's coming and he's bringing with him a very handsome young man."

"Isn't it odd," said Adela, "I still remember what I wore,

the care I took getting dressed. A green silk blouse with hand-drawn threads and tucks on it, a grey skirt, and black silk stockings to show an ankle.

"The young man seemed to have fallen in love with the King, my father. Well, that didn't surprise me. As you know I worshipped him myself. The young man had seen a picture of me looking about thirteen, with my hair down, a photo my father carried with him on his travels. He said to my father: 'I should like to meet that girl.' 'She is my daughter,' said my father. And then: 'I will introduce you.'

"It is true they rode a long way together, crossing valleys and mountain streams and the borders of several countries, but there was nothing wonderful about the meeting. He seemed a formal, rather proud young man. And not so young at that. He was over thirty, and had made his way in life. He, too, had been born in Poland, in a different part, and now lived in Germany, where it was obvious he'd made his pile. It seemed I was desirable in his eyes because I was the daughter of such a man. He had made it clear to my father that he was looking for a wife."

The heart which beat in the well-developed, low-slung bosom of the young princess had not been captured. She prepared to return to her endless game of cards. Enter two neighbourly ladies-in-waiting, breathless and shrieking. Two droshkies packed with flowers were coming down the street, like a garden, moving. Followed, it seemed by the strange young man. He'd emptied the contents of all three flower shops in the little town. He'd had to hire an extra droshky to travel in.

On the piano, on the floor, on stairs and window sills, in bottles and jam jars and tureens. There were flowers everywhere. And behind the flowers, a trifle smug, awaiting the result, her suitor. Well, she'd dreamed of this. Hadn't they all, every last silly spoilt princess of them? She looked at the young man. Perhaps all that reserve, that smug exterior, hid depths as yet unplumbed? A romantic gesture, yet he seemed an unromantic man. A puzzle. Was that irony in the set of his mouth, or raising that fine brow? He looked at her across the flowers. Outside, maidens twittered in the twilight.

"I'd like to take you out," he said.

And so she walked with him, sedately, the next day, at an appropriate hour in the late afternoon.

It was difficult to talk. "You were very extravagant," she said, "about the flowers."

"They came with me, your two friends," he told her simply. "It was their idea. They stood with me in the flower shops. Buy this, buy that. I never learned anything at home about flowers. I could not tell a peony from a tomato plant. In the end they said, if you really want to impress her, if you want to win Adela, buy her the lot. *Drench* her in flowers. So then we hired the carts."

Why did she not turn back at that very moment, or turn on him? Why not? This man was no romantic, wooing *her*. This was a man of means who was looking for a wife. But the flowers had done their trick, she had been impressed, and now here she was walking with this stranger, rigid in his best suit and his best behaviour, allowing him to guide her through the town she knew so well. Well, he was generous, at least. She could never marry an ungenerous man. They passed a *parfumerie* displaying a mammoth bottle of "Quelques Fleurs". "I'll buy you that," he said grandly. Her heart soared. She had not been wrong. This prince would win her at whatever price. "I'll bring you one from Germany next month. The prices there are better." Should she have dropped his arm? Do you drop the arm of such a cavalier because of petty meanness? Because of a bottle of "Quelques Fleurs?"

Then the droshky. Oh, the droshky. Yes. They'd had coffee and pastries and more coffee. The conversation had been plainer than the cakes, but who'd notice that when his eyes never left you? What if persons not a million miles away had admired her hair, her eyes, her profile or the angle of her head? This man admired her father and the grace in her which spoke of him. It was one of those old patisseries smelling of chocolate and vanilla and cinnamon and that whiff of waitress sweat which used to excite her elder brothers so, and they came out of it into a light summer rain. Oh, the intimacy! An umbrella opened. An arm taken. Twilight deepening. A droshky to drive them gently home.

She knew them all, of course, horses and drivers, from her early childhood. Jacob approached one and she started up the steps. He held her back, and in his lordly tones, enquired – that such a thing could be! – enquired the price. Worse, argued, *haggled* for a price! Is this the way to drive a princess home? No worthy princeling he. A bourgeois from the depths of bourgeoisie. Into a bargain droshky, then, she climbed, but his steady arm, creeping around her as they rattled home, did nothing to steady her strung nerves. She had been *warned*. And now?

The village, the castle, the court, the King her father expected it. She knew the role. She saw herself enacting it. Radiant, she'd step from the droshky at the door, a modest diamond larger than a pigeon's egg, weighing her slender hand. Applause. Instead, she said a stiff goodnight, and fled.

All night she sat weeping in the rocking chair, rocking and keening. The child's gone mad, they said. It had been known in other fairy tales. Excitement. The intrusion of the dangerous real world. The threat of having to venture into it, away from home. The thunderous power of love had robbed the odd princess or two of sanity. Giselle, name of her mother and of her aunt the painter who had run away to Paris. Rock, weep, rock. "Nobody says you have to marry him. If you don't want to marry him, don't marry him, my darling, my baby girl. Adela, Adelaida, Adeloushka. I'm not pushing you away. I'll send him packing."

"But I knew, you see, that times were lean in the kingdom, and my beloved father was in trouble. A princess is expected to make a good match, to get lands and gold to help her father and redeem the realm. And this young man was rich. After the revolution of '17 we Poles went to war with Russia for our independence, and we won. But of course our savings became completely worthless. Everyone's did. My father showed us a trunkful of paper money. Czarist currency. Alas, the Czar was dead. 'Children,' he told us, 'we are poor.' The tea and coffee merchant owed us a lot of money, so he paid us a sack of tea and a sack of coffee. 'You see, father,' we told him, 'everyone's poor.'"

"Viktusia, our maid, who'd saved us from so many pogroms, hiding us in cupboards, barricading doors, shouting sturdily at them in her country voice, 'What do you want? There's only me, Viktusia, here,' and, adding a curse or two in dialect, Viktusia went off her head. She'd worked all her life to provide for the child she doted on, born of her first job in a big country house, illegitimately, of course. What had happened to her money, her life's work? She could not understand. My father had saved a sum for her each year, a pension, he'd told her, to take care of her old age. And now? She thought my father a liar or a thief.

"There was worse to come for father. His workers turned against him, his own men, hunting him down with pitchforks, calling vengeance on him in the name of his boss. Father was forced to hide under a bed. He never ceased trembling from that day." Her smiling father, her dignified, urbane, well-travelled father, that calming presence, scrupulously fair, was never to be seen again. The man who emerged from under that bed was none of these, but a trembling old man.

The princess felt such pity in her breast, such hurt. She must do everything in her power to help. Her elder brothers had, by now, left home, the youngest was too young, and so it fell to her. She must stop this fooling with romantic Poles or boys she could love and want to help, and sell herself to the highest bidder, a man so rich he wouldn't take a dowry. Was this the man?

"We will put him to the test," she said. She instructed her father carefully in her wishes. "Do not give him a penny, father. I am not in love."

"Their meeting was to be at the railway station. When father came back he kissed me and said, 'You are engaged'."

"Am I indeed? I thought it was a test. Will he take me in one skirt?

"My father hesitated just a beat too long. 'You know I had a sum put by for you and he'll take that – for the furniture.'

"I was truly frightened then for the first time. It was all a big mistake.

"'You betrayed me, father,' I told him.

"Well, Jacob didn't take the dowry, that is true. He told my father graciously he didn't need it. But then, oh, then, he uttered those fateful words which have rankled fifty years. 'Well, if you want to help us, sir,' he said, 'and it's very kind of you, most kind, you could help us towards our house. I want to give her the best of everything.'

"'Why did you take my father's money,' I kept on. 'Were you *buying* me?' He never answered this. He smiled his ironical small smile which could have meant anything. I was confused, you see. I was the bartered bride. But was I being bought or sold? It wasn't clear. Yet rules had been obeyed. What followed seemed inexorable. A bargain had been struck without my aid – this castle for those lands, and I to exile. Germany. Another country, another home, a language I had only learned at school. A new name, a new status, new loneliness. Instead of my family, my friends, my neighbours, this stranger I had met a week ago.

"Well, then I married him and went away. He put me in a beautiful flat in a tree-lined street in Dusseldorf. I could not complain. The sheets were linen and the monograms handworked, the carpets Persian silk. There were crystal chandeliers. My portrait was painted, my Bechstein grand piano duly bought. Locked in my tower alone I played the ivories and waited. So this was married life?

"My husband moved mysteriously in this strange new world and seemed to know everything we should or should not do. We were completely kitted out for all occasions. A box at the Opera? I had a shawl of saffron coloured silk, a golden handbag with a jewelled clasp, mother of pearl opera glasses in a small green velvet bag. Skiing in the Tyrol? Here's a snapshot: Jacob in tweed plus-fours. We had fur lined travelling capes. Our luggage was pale cream hide so fine it had covers of brown linen, leather piped. It was monogrammed, of course, and lined inside with moiré. Every winter we went skiing in St Moritz and every summer we went to a summer spa. Kissingen or Baden Baden. Nice or the Venice Lido. Each holiday was four weeks long.

"And when we weren't travelling, I sat in my 'capella', (a pretty word, it means a chapel) all alone, and wondered what I should do to be a wife. Should I make a soufflé. I who had never boiled an egg? Should I roast a goose? Once, I asked a neighbour how to make fruit salad. You take six oranges, she said, six apples, six bananas. I followed her instructions to the letter. My hands shook as I lifted the heavy crystal bowl on to the table. Only then did the question of quantity occur to me. There was enough for a celebration. But who did we know well enough to invite? And what could we celebrate?

"It mattered not. My husband noticed nothing, neither my lack of commonsense, nor my fine accomplishments. I played waltzes, mazurkas. No one danced. There was no one to talk to in the languages I knew. And there were things he did which irritated me: signs, as I thought, of middle age, like wearing galoshes every time it rained, and fussing with hats and umbrellas as an old man would. Worse, he took sandwiches to eat in the intervals at the opera. I was shocked by that. I thought if he really loved me, or the music, he should live on air. I was too young to know then that you can be hungry and in love. And besides, it lacked style. A young man would buy chocolates and take you out to supper afterwards. Anyway, I did my best. I posed elegantly as I could in our box at the theatre, my hand on the good pearls at my throat. But by this time he knew the truth: I hated opera. He had yet to guess, as I boarded one more train or boat or ski lift, how I hated travelling. Nothing mattered. Once he had locked me in that tower of his, we never touched, because he never touched me."

9

A weekend at Rupert and Serena's country house was a weekend in another world: a honey-coloured stone Folly set in thirty green and undulating acres, Serena was systematically restoring it to a glory it had never known. Sarah and David entered by the Conservatory, which was not the thing to do. Assorted figures languished behind virile looking plants. The hellos were inaudible, as usual, the introductions unintelligible. Who were Snooks and Badger, anyway? And did we care? As usual, everyone was Someone, other than oneself, but one would only discover who, after Sunday lunch, at departure time, when the full extent of one's *gaffes* would be revealed.

A small Hon, a replica of Rupert, detached himself from the strings of a kite and approached David.

"There's a whole family of dead hedgehogs at the end of the kitchen garden," he said gleefully, tugging at David's hand. "Want to see? They won't be there tomorrow 'cos we're going to bury them. We're going to have a funeral."

"Can I, Mummy?"

"Yes, you *may*. But only if you put some wellies on first. Do you remember where they are, the wellies? Inside the outer kitchen door?"

As they disappeared, a figure uncurled itself from a cane chair suspended from the ceiling, stretched like a lazy lion, and advanced towards Sarah.

"Well . . ."

"Jonathan! I had no idea you'd be here!"

"You never can tell!" He kissed her on both cheeks and whispered into her ear: "I see me son's bloomin'".

"He is, rather," said Sarah.

Later, over the cucumber sandwiches, nearly all of which were eaten by someone predictably named Algy, they were formally introduced.

"Aren't you the lady I met before in the conservatory? Gwendolen, wasn't it?"

"Sarah," said Sarah. "And you? Are you related to the quite famous playwright of the same name?"

"Any resemblance between me and characters with the same name is not merely accidental, it's entirely fictitious."

"Do you think they *know*?" she whispered.

"Who? Polly? Never knows anything. Believes what she reads in *Private Eye*."

"I thought it was all written here, anyway, each weekend."

David came up and hugged Sarah tightly at hip level.

"Mummy, we're going to have a funeral. Will you come?"

"If you insist," said Sarah.

"Did you see the hedgehogs?" Jonathan asked him.

"Yes."

"What were they like?"

"They were dead."

They looked at each other out of the same candid eyes. With a pang Sarah realized she had no idea exactly what they saw. The look excluded her. Oh, God, what had she done? They belonged together, and it could never be.

Over the before dinner Scotch, an American said, "I heard the kids telling the most appalling joke, and then I discovered it had been launched on the scene by my own son. It goes like this: there were two carrots on motorbikes going very fast. They crashed and were squashed – all over the sidewalk. The ambulance came and took them to hospital, where they went to work to try to save them. After a while the doctors came out and said they would live. Now that's the good news, they said. The bad news is" – he paused impressively – "they'll always be vegetables."

"Wow," said Jonathan. "I need another drink."

Rupert made an entrance in a rather snazzy tartan dinner jacket, and behind him sailed his mother-in-law, a stately galleonic version of Serena, who followed and announced that dinner was served.

"Behind every great man stands a great woman," said Jonathan. A man with a portrait of Groucho knitted into his sweater grinned at him. "And behind *her* stands his wife," said the man, finishing the joke. Jonathan could have sworn that the eye of the knitted Groucho winked at him.

The company moved to the dining room and began talking about who was still with whom and whether Polly or Molly or Nigel or Boof or even Candida would be the one to leave next.

"I'm thinking of doing a play called 'Sinister Couples'," said Jonathan, grinning at Sarah.

"What does it mean?" asked the one called Algy.

"Oh, it doesn't *mean* anything. A sinister couple is where one person assimilates the other."

"A murder story?"

"Perhaps." Dropping the level of his voice to a near whisper, Jonathan held the attention of the table. "How many couples do you know where there are really two people there?" He raised his voice again. "These are matters which cannot be spoken of out loud."

"One person has a life and the other shares it," said Sarah into the silence.

"What's that?" asked Jonathan, leaning forward across the candles.

"Something a woman said to me once about the state of marriage. Tell me, if there aren't two people there, what happens if one of them dies?"

He beamed at her. "You're on to it . . . clever girl."

"Those two are a couple," someone said. "Look at them, flirting over the candles. She even understands what he says . . ."

"We're not a couple, Sarah and I," said Jonathan, enjoying himself. "We're a pigeon pair."

Knock, knock.

Who's there?

Sarah.

Sarah who?

S'ere a doctor in the house?

"Like it? I got it from your son before he went to bed." Jonathan kicked Sarah's bedroom door shut behind him, and, somehow holding a steaming champagne bottle and two glasses in one hand, grabbed Sarah and hugged her to him with the other.

"You're a terrific girl. No wonder I made you pregnant." He flopped on the bed and started to pour the champagne. "I opened this in the loo. I thought someone might hear us popping it in here, and there – well, it might be a fart." He cast his glance heavenward. "Cor, it's a bit frilly, your four poster."

"It's not meant for blokes." She stretched out alongside him and took the proffered glass.

"Now I've seen your four poster, would you like to see mine?"

"It's seven years since you made me pregnant. Every cell in my body has changed."

"What's that supposed to mean?"

"I don't know." She giggled and bubbles went up her nose. "I've got an idea for you for a play. On the theme we began to discuss downstairs."

"I'll steal it if it's any good."

"You can't if I give it to you. It's based on the Alcestis of Euripides. Do you know the story? Death comes for King Admetus but he doesn't want to die. So his wife, Alcestis says to him, 'Never mind, darling,' she says, 'I'll die for you'."

"Go on," said Jonathan, pouring more champagne.

"Well, she bargains with Death, who accepts the swop somewhat grudgingly and she goes into the Dark – Hades, to be exact. But the natural order must be restored – her sacrifice has a six month lease on it, as I remember. After that, no one can make out what was meant to happen. There's a bit where she goes round her house saying goodbye to everything and apostrophizing like mad, you know: 'Farewell, oh bed on which I lost my maidenhood!' You can imagine how we tittered over that at school. But if you put it in modern dress, it's the ultimate sacrifice a wife can make for her husband. Only one degree greater than what most wives do, anyway. It asks all the questions. Cunning old thing, Euripides."

"Yeth," lipsed Jonathan, hamming it up shamelessly in his best camp voice. "She wath a feminitht. You can alwayth tell."

His eyes grew misty. "I can see it all . . . I'll die for you . . ." he crooned. "If you'll die for me . . . There's this handsome, weary, brittle couple, Anthony and Alice Admetus. They have a flat above the Park (Hyde or Central as the case may be). The action takes place a day or so after Alice has returned from a brief trip to Paris. Anthony has suffered a (first) mild heart attack and is in bed. Alice is obviously riddled with guilt that this has happened while she was away. She protests a lot to Anthony that she had to get some frocks, so we suspect her. Anthony is extremely upset, and although the attack was not a serious one, takes it as an Awful Warning. 'I can't afford to die now,' he says. 'There's the Multinational Whatsit contract coming up . . .'"

"And Death, who comes for him, is of course, the doctor," Sarah says.

"That's it. Knock knock."

"Who's there?"

"Doctor Who?"

"No. Doctor Death."

"Your very own Thanatory Inspector."

"Complete with his sinister black Gallstone bag."

"A *hand* bag . . ."

They fell about on the bed, laughing and burping champagne.

Suddenly Sarah sat up. "You're on the wrong side – that's my side of the bed if you don't mind."

He tweaked her robe and it fell apart.

"I saw the bush!"

She tossed her head. "And was it burning?"

He bent down and kissed it softly. "Just smouldering," he said. "Here, let's finish the bubbly. Admetus says sulkily: 'This wouldn't have happened if you'd been here. When we met, you said you'd do anything for me, Alice. I remember. You said you'd die for me.'

'No, you said that to me,' says Alice firmly.

Anthony is startled. 'I did?'

'Yes, you did,' says Alice. 'You said you'd die unless I went to bed with you. You said it was very bad for men to frustrate their sexual drive. You said you could die of it.'

Anthony, defensively: 'Well, we were very young. The point is I can't die now, and you can't let me die . . .'"

Jonathan drained the bottle, then dropped it into the wastepaper basket. "Well, that's dead. I thought of writing a play about Nadezhda Mandelstam. A fantastic woman. Have you read her books? She actually became her husband by committing every word of every poem of his to memory. They took him away and he died, poor bastard, but he was not dead. She wouldn't let him die. Her memory was his survival. Through her he became immortal. And the best thing of all was, that when she was sure he would survive, she became herself again: she was free to become herself. And Nadezhda's self was an indomitable self. But for as long as he needed her, she was there for him: she was a house in which her husband dwelt."

Sarah blinked blurrily at him. "Why is it always the man who becomes immortal and the woman who survives?"

She looked at their long straight limbs stretched out alongside one another. "We are a couple, you know."

"We're not. We're a pigeon pair." He kissed her. She burped and he laughed. "That's enough from you. Now, go to sleep."

All day long the memory of how they had laughed and lain together, touching and not touching, remained with her, adding warmth to the pale sunshine and the soothing country house routine. Breakfast was eaten, long walks were taken, renovations to the house admired. Shepherds Pie and Rhubarb Fool were consumed in quantity. Children and animals were introduced to one another, and adults afforded ample opportunity to avoid each other. By twilight, the air around Sarah seemed to tingle, her skin tingled, her senses tingled. There was a name for this, she knew, and the name was Expectancy. Six o'clock. Drinks were poured. Baths run. Off in the kitchen, no concern of hers, dinner was being prepared. In the nursery wing children were being fed and bathed and put to bed. She peeped in on David, who was earnestly absorbed in stuffing mashed potato into a small girl's neighbouring mouth. Well, she'd take a leisurely bath before dinner.

Her beautiful room was cool and welcoming, her bathroom an Aladdin's cave of enchantment, every shelf and ledge crammed with exotic fragrances, and expensive pampery. She ran her bath and sniffed from all the bottles. Essence of fern and forest, of herbs and flowers and fields enveloped her. Spices and wood scents and strange smoky smells. Overripe whiffs of orient and orange. Waxy magnolia, gardenia . . . what shall she choose? She caressed a woman-shaped bottle, sniffed the stopper and filled the bath with bubbles. She unwrapped a new bar of curved soap which fitted her hand, and slipped down the length of her body, as caresses do. The bathroom steamed up, but the breeze from the open window billowed the curtains and touched her wet skin. She shivered deliciously. A sultry night, moon coming up, wind rustling the trees. Her face flooded with colour from the heat of the bath. She'd run it too hot, as usual. Damp tendrils of hair clung to her neck and her forehead. She cleared a circular space in the steamed up mirror and peered at herself: a woman waiting.

Shall she have lotion and talc? Perhaps talc by itself might be better tonight. And scent, of course, lots of it, everywhere, in all the secret and unlikely places. Her bath robe flew open as she walked into her bedroom, the wind touching her intimately. She lay damply on a velvet *chaise longue* by the open window, feeling the texture of the velvet prickle her bottom and her back. The wind stirred her pubic hairs. For a while she abandoned herself to the wind, head thrown back, throat raised. Later there would be moonlight. She got up in a trance and tried to concentrate. Now, let's see. This long, clinging number will do. No bra. Knickers? The line will show. No knickers. Delicate high shoes. Earrings. A bracelet. A ring. The inside curves at the top of her thighs brushed each other as she walked downstairs, making a gentle sucking sound, skin on skin. How would she get through dinner?

The chair legs curved, the velvet seat caressed. She leaned her bare back against smooth carved wood and focused slowly. Her lashes blurred the light but she did not have to look to know. His eyes would meet hers now, this moment, across the candle flames. They did. He raised one eyebrow slightly at her. Blond hairs on his hand shivered as he raised his glass. The pulse in her throat began to throb with such insistency she was sure it could be heard. She watched the tips of his fingers go white on the ice cold glass he held. The sharp, exquisite stabs of pain began, like needles of silk, of grass, of fern. Like needles.

Alone again in her room, she leaned faintly against the door. It opened. He locked it from the inside. He picked her up. He carried her, ceremoniously, to the bed. He was here, there, everywhere. At last. He was into every corner, every cranny, every nook of her. A rhythm insistent as the sea took over, a rhythm which lapped her, lulled her, roared in her ears. Don't stop, oh, please don't stop. He didn't. The waves rose up and sucked her under, till she woke, and drowned.

Years later, he heard her murmuring happily to herself.

"Did you say something?"

"Only – it always seems so simple with you."

"What does?"

"Oh, making love. Being happy. Little things like that."

"You can't believe in them, can you?"

"What?"

"Simplicity. Everything's got to be complex for you. That way you work so hard for it, you might even deserve it."

"That's not fair. I've got a great talent for happiness. You ought to know..." She stretched herself. "What I'd really like is to eliminate everything in my life except making love like this and writing our play."

"I'd take you up on that, my lady. You're on. If and when you can unload your four hundred and sixty nine Responsibilities . . ."

Jonathan fell asleep with his arms still round her. They had left the curtains open and bars of moonlight lay across the bed. She could hear the wind stirring the trees but it was no longer a restless sound. Far off across the woods an owl hooted. She wondered if David heard it in his sleep. She moved slightly, and Jonathan's arms tightened instinctively. She smiled to herself: "the lovers, their arms round the griefs of the ages". She turned towards Jonathan, and slept, too.

10

Mel dipped her toes in the shallow end of a large municipal swimming pool in the open, if not fresh, South London air, where David and seven other six and seven year olds were competing noisily.

"Oh, I love swimming pools," she said rapturously. "All the shouting! Here – look after the things for me. I can't resist. I must go in."

She thrust a motley collection of towels with knickers and shirts and shoes rolled up in them at Sarah and vanished into a cubicle to change. Sarah sat down on the cracked concrete ground and leaned her back gingerly against a powdery wall. The towels fell in piles around her, spilling treasures everywhere. Wet children rushed at her to grab a towel, a biscuit, a comb, shaking themselves all over her like puppies. The noise, even in the open, was deafening, the smell of chlorine sickening, the surroundings ugly. Mel returned glowing from her dip as if she'd just immersed herself in the balmiest of southern seas and been handed a long cool drink by a suntanned man. Two small boys clung to her, one on either side, while a small girl squirted her behind rudely with a broken water wing.

"What do you get if you cross an elephant with a goldfish?"

Sarah shook her head.

"Swimming trunks," chorused the children.

As required of her, Sarah groaned.

Mel dried an assortment of limbs, her own included, with inadequate small towels, and continued the diatribe she'd begun that morning.

"I still don't know what you think you're proving with these Fast Ladies of yours. I'm not convinced."

Sarah groaned again.

"They were all privileged, those old birds. Admit it. I mean they all came from privileged backgrounds, didn't they? And not one single one of them, as far as I can see, was independent. It's back to Virginia Woolf visiting the kitchen to discuss the soufflé with that cook who wrote about her. Or that other old bag, Violet whatsername, going to see her great love, Vita, and stepping over the woman who was scrubbing the steps."

"I know, I know. You'd give anything for the diary of the woman scrubbing the steps."

"Haven't you got any interesting working class women?"

"No. But I can offer you the first woman trade union official, who lived to be over a hundred."

"That's better," said Mel.

"Aha, caught you. You think she must be working class. Well, I'm not sure about that. She was a Yorkshire woman whose father was a sculptor called Canova Throp. I don't know what that makes her. Can working class men be named for Canova in your book. Or working class women for

Fidelio? Mind you, Canova Throp did inherit his skill from *his* father, who was a monumental stone mason. Honestly, Mel, you're so predictable, you're getting to be a parody of yourself. Everything about you betrays you as middle class, down to the Georgian style dolls' house you keep for the children to play with."

Mel had the grace to laugh. "What could I do? They don't make any others."

"I'm surprised. You'd think there would be some place down in Camden Lock making trendy slum dolls' houses for trendy Left families."

"It's quite a thought. They'd do a roaring trade. I might go in for it myself. Dustbins and dry rot and racist graffiti all over the walls... I should have kept my own childhood dolls' house. At least it was only ordinary northern suburban, pebble dash."

"Gabled? Detached? Stop fighting it, Mel. It's not a disgrace to be born middle class. Relax. Stop hanging your good paintings in the kitchen and your posters in the drawing room. You're a classist, and that's just as bad as being racist or sexist, don't you see?"

She watched Mel struggle damply into her dress. "Look at the girl. She even wears Liberty lawn. You can tell just by looking at her that she practises her Czerny piano studies every morning."

"Enough," said Mel. "You've got a point. So have I. Admit it. All your ancient ladies have in common is their laugh."

"Trust you to notice that," Sarah said. "I do go on a bit about their laughs. Except for Jean Rhys. Who only smiled. And Julia. Who didn't even smile. But had you thought?

Laughter could be a factor in survival. It keeps people young."

They piled the children into Mel's battered car and careered top-heavily down the road. A boy who turned out to be a girl called Jennifer wanted to sit on David's knee and he fought her off energetically till the car swerved to a final stop at McDonald's, the little children's mecca.

"How do you get four elephants into a mini?" screamed the children, disentangling their limbs and climbing out of the car. "Give up?"

A collective giggle. "Two in the front and two in the back."

How else?

Hamburgers were "disintegrated", french fries and ketchup "pulverized", milkshakes "vaporized."

"How do you know if there's an elephant hiding in the fridge?"

"Footprints in the butter."

Mel and Sarah finished the leftovers with relish of both kinds.

"Dustbins, our destiny," said Mel.

"Independent dustbins?"

"How does an elephant hide in the custard?"

"Paints the soles of his feet yellow and goes to sleep upside down."

"You'll be sick."

"I was sick last night. I went yuk, yuk, all over the place and my mum had to mop it up."

"I was sick every night when I was little. My cot smelled

horrible. My mum went yuk, yuk when she smelled it. And then my sister was sick . . ."

Mel seemed unmoved. "What you need in that series are some stalwart ladies who've suffered the heavy domestic life, like Tillie Olsen. Remember that story of hers, *I Stand Here Ironing*?"

"If I stand here any longer I'll be sick."

Once more they all piled into Mel's car.

"Who was the lady trade union leader?" asked the indefatigable Mel.

ENCOUNTERS/ENCOUNTERS

Leonora Cohen, CBE, was a Yorkshire woman, born Leonora Throp, in Leeds, in 1873. She became one of the most militant of the suffragettes, and lived to be over a hundred years old, despite much damage to her person and a spell in Armley Jail. In 1918 she walked into the Tower of London with an iron bar concealed in her clothing and smashed a domed glass display of the Crown Jewels. "I was terrified," she remembered at the age of ninety-three. "I hate violence and destruction. To this day I can't think how I managed to do such a thing. I caught the underground to Mark Lane with this iron bar three of us had cut from a fire grate, wrapped in a piece of paper, but I was so frightened I could not get out of the train and had to go round again." Finally, she did the deed, a Beefeater grabbed her and she was arrested.

As personal bodyguard to Mrs Pankhurst, she expected violence. "I used to wrap myself in an undercovering of corrugated brown paper for protection. On one deputation to the House of Commons, I was knocked over and rolled under the hooves of the police horses. Over three hundred of us were taken to Bow Street. I was given a week in Holloway." When Prime Minister Asquith ("Wait-and-see Asquith we called him") came to speak in Leeds, Leonora hurled a brick through a window and finished up going on a hunger and thirst strike in Armley Jail. "I'm still only out on licence," she chuckled on her hundredth birthday. "I've seen the entry at Armley: Leonora Cohen, Temporary Discharge.

"I have always been appalled by injustice. My mother was left a widow with me and my two brothers to bring up, all of us very young. Life was hard. My mother would often say: 'Leonora, if only we women had a say in things.' But we hadn't. A drunken lout of a man opposite had a vote simply because he was a male. I vowed I'd try to change things. I felt it in my bones.

"My mother was a great influence on me. 'It's no use your arguing about which party you'll vote for when you're grown,' she'd say to me. 'You'll never have the vote.' I grew up wanting to prove her wrong. She cradled my interest in the vote for women. But I never dreamt we'd get it, you know. There was so much male supremacy in every department and profession."

Once, Leonora and her mother went together to a meeting of suffragettes on Harrogate's Stray. A mob thrust into the crowd and broke up the meeting, smashing the platform and hitting the women. Her mother was attacked, had her thumb broken, and died soon afterwards.

Leonora's father, sculptor Canova Throp, died of tuberculosis of the spine at the age of "nine and twenty", when Leonora was only five. As a small child Leonora suffered the same disease that killed her father. It kept her away from school until she was past seven. At ninety, Leonora appealed to the Council to save her father's monumental stone sculpture of King Stephen and his horsemen on the Royal Exchange Building, City Square, Leeds. The sculpture depicts King Stephen's siege of Leeds Castle in 1139, and was the culmination of Canova Throp's short lifetime's work.

During the Great War, Leonora earned one pound a week for a fifty-two hour week in an ammunition factory, became a member of the Leeds Food Control Council, and practised as a magistrate.

In 1922 she went to Germany to investigate industrial conditions in the Black Forest, and was much shaken by the sadness of the people, their poverty, the "pathetic" clothes she saw hanging out to dry, which were so patched, she said, hardly any of the original garments were left. On a workmen's train men munched steadily at their black bread with "nothing whatever on it to make it palatable". People in factories were resigned to hopelessness. "Posters admonishing you to work stare you in the face at every turn. I hope I shall never live to see the day when the working classes of England have to keep their noses to the grindstone as have the Germans I saw at work in the Black Forest," she said. And added: "But I have come to the conclusion that the psychology of the Britisher is so vastly different from the psychology of the Germans that it is almost useless trying to compare the two peoples."

In 1923 Leonora was the first woman to be elected President of the Yorkshire Federation of Trade Councils, and the Leeds Trades and Labour Council. "A very able and esteemed Trade Union Official is Mrs Leonora Cohen," wrote the *Yorkshire Evening News* in September 1927 when she retired as President, under a portrait of Leonora as a level-headed beauty with clear, steady eyes and firm mouth. "In the days of women's suffrage, she was the honorary secretary of the now defunct Women's Social and Political Union. During the Great War she was the only woman member of the Leeds Food Control Committee. It will thus be seen that Mrs Cohen has blazed the trail for many other women. She is now district organiser of the Union of General and Municipal Workers and devotes a good deal of time to magisterial duties."

In her retiring speech as President, Leonora referred to "recent recriminations between trade union leaders", and said there was an attempt by those within their own ranks to smash the workers' organizations. "The cancerous growth of Communism must have its causations diagnosed and early treatment before the disease spread all over the body in malignant form destroying the whole structure of the trade union movement."

A voice: Tommy Rot.

"Yes, you say rot when it is against you," said the President.

In 1927 Leonora went on an official visit to Canada, and voted it "one of the most interesting things I have ever done in my life". As District Organizer of the National Union of General and Municipal Workers, she accompanied a party of fifty emigrants, most of them going out to domestic service, and the reception they got was the first surprise which awaited her. "Getting maids over there is like getting tea in wartime," she reported. The demand was such they could earn as much as thirty dollars a month. "You will have seen that Mr Baldwin says 'What Canada needs is men and money', and that when he says 'men' he means men and women. I have always been strongly opposed to emigration for women because I did not know what the conditions were. But now that I have seen them, I can conscientiously say – and with all my heart and soul, if that would make it stronger – that there is a grand opening for women in Canada, and I would defy anybody to say otherwise. I refer especially to domestic occupations. Waitresses, for instance, start at twelve dollars fifty a week.

"There is an atmosphere out there that is youthful and virile and infectious; and one doesn't wonder when one realizes the immense spaciousness of the country and how little concerned they are with what we regard as tradition. Then, too, the resources of the country are so amazing. The climate is glorious, vegetation is luxuriant, the land contains great mineral wealth, and the water is there for the generation of vast electric power. All this is waiting for man power and brain power to develop it. And the point is," Leonora added with a touch of pride, "it is a British Dominion. One felt a glowing touch of kinship in the way they always spoke of us as the Mother Country. I loved that. And if the Mother Country is worked to death, and it is time she had a rest, then in Canada is our future. I am convinced of it. For young people, Canada is the place to go to."

On her hundredth birthday Leonora was still in Britain, in Wales to be exact. A serene, white haired old lady, she rose every day at seven, did all her own cooking and was a strict vegetarian, always baking her own wholemeal bread. It was not ever thus. "I'm afraid I was a terrible worry to my husband. He was most patient, kind and understanding. He gave up a lot to marry me . . ." Henry Cohen was cut off with a shilling by his family when he married Leonora. He was Jewish. She was not. But he did not care. "The family problems only pushed us closer together. We had a very happy life together," Leonora said.

When he died, in 1949, Henry Cohen left a tribute to Leonora in his will: I have lived in perfect appreciation of all her loving and unselfish devotion throughout our happy life together. My love for her has been the one perfect happiness that life has given to me.

11

Adam was back. Sarah and David sat on the bed as he unpacked, both of them bouncing with glee as the presents appeared from the depths of his bags. Perfume and ethnic jewellery and a caftan for Sarah; carved and polished soapstone animals for David; carved wooden warriors and a terrifying mask; an embroidered shirt in exactly David's size. His cupboard shelves filled up again with immaculate hotel-laundered shirts, each in its cellophane wrapper. Sand streaked the carpet as he put his shoes away.

"I have to spend three days in New York," Sarah said. "I thought I'd go next week."

Adam made a face. "I'm only just back."

"That's the point. I couldn't have gone while you were away. I like David to have one of us here all the time."

"I like you to be here when I'm here," Adam said. "We're apart enough." He disappeared into the shower.

"That's hardly my fault," Sarah muttered.

"What did you say?" he shouted above the water.

"Nothing."

Adam emerged again, dressed like a young executive. He picked up his briefcase, sorted some papers, stood up.

"You're not going out again, now?"

"Why not? It's only eleven here. I've got an amazing amount to do."

"Besides, the legions must report to Rome?"

"Something like that," he kissed the top of her head. "We'll talk about your trip later. Can't be necessary, can it?"

He was gone.

This time Adam had been gone six weeks. Sometimes it was as much as twelve. She had had to get used to it. She had had to cope. And just as she began to feel adult and in control, and to like the sense of responsibility, the sense of running her own life, the freedom, Adam came back and she was dependent again: a small girl at his beck and call. To think that he assumed she was *asking* him if she could go away for three days, a necessity for her job, when all these years she had prided herself on never once whining, or questioning or showing by so much as a headache or a grimace that she minded him leaving her regularly for as long as three months! With a start Sarah realized that she had never imposed her will on her husband about anything at all, big or small, in the whole of their married life. She loaded the dirty socks into the washing machine. There was a first time for everything, she supposed.

Precariously, Sarah perched on the edge of the plastic covered seat as the yellow cab careened between cemeteries and clapboard houses, poised for the moment, that first moment when she would see the skyline. Those cloud-capped towers, those gorgeous palaces, that urban fairy tale. New York. The impossible dream. And there it was again, misty against the glow of early evening light, glimmering seductively, every glimmer an electric promise it will fail to keep. Her spirits soared to around the height of the spire of the Chrysler building, still her favourite, and she knew from experience they would stay there till the trip was done.

"I'm in love with the New York skyline," she'd confessed in breathless tones every day of that first working trip to the big, big Apple. "Well, honey," someone said, with a look more amused than askance, "you've sure chosen the most phallic apparition in the modern world." Be that as it may, New York had remained the Big High for Sarah. It always worked.

The cockroaches and the rusty bathwater and the familiar black servants welcomed her to the crumbling mid-town Manhattan hostelry she always stayed at. The central heating coughed, the air-conditioning spluttered. A chunk of discoloured plaster fell off the ceiling as she stepped into the shower. The water was soft and the town was hard as the thousand feet of granite it stood upon. No matter. She'd conquer it. She'd just spent seven hours cramped in a space capsule. So what! The night was young and she was going to a party.

The party took place in what seemed like an enormous hangar and was to launch a new feminist magazine called *Emerging*, which had said that it wanted to publish some but not all the Fast Ladies. Inside the hangar were the most extraordinary collection of people you could hope to see. Girls dressed as boys and men dressed as women, there was every style on parade from Sappho to punk, and the maximum amount of gender confusion you could engender in one room. How she wished Adrian were here! Nervously adjusting the bow tie she'd borrowed from Adam, she peered about her, espying people she knew and trying to make her way over to them through the crush.

A twenty-one piece, all-female Brass Band called The Sisterhood of Spit had come over from England especially to blast in the occasion and bust a few ear drums.

There was that special New York buzz of excitement in the air: something new was happening in a city which thrives on the new. There was that feeling that "everyone" was there, though since about seventy-five percent of the company looked female, it seemed unlikely that this was the case. And there was nothing new about the faces, either. In a corner, flanked by her large black protectress, Gladys, and a circle of admirers, Sarah saw Anita Loos, whom she was due to interview next day. Eighty-seven years old and well under five feet small, Miss Loos still made her presence felt. Sarah was hailed by Geraldine, ("call me Gerry") the editor of *Emerging* who was declaring loudly that she had been celibate for four years and eleven days, and by an enchanting black slip of a thing called Charlotte, ("call me Charlie"), in leg warmers and not much else, who was in charge of features.

She had three separate reunions with three of her old school friends, each holding down an amazing topline job: one in newspapers, one in advertising, and one at the United Nations. Two women had a fight, which gratified the press and caused screams of horror and delight. Dresses and hair were torn, spectacles stamped upon, shoes unheeled. When enough photos had been taken the contestants were pulled apart. Felicity, who was to run *Emerging*'s problem page appeared by Sarah's side.

"Want to go home?" she asked. "You've gotta be utterly jet-lagged by now. It's five a.m. in London. Come, I'll take you home."

In the taxi, Felicity took her hand. "You can call me Phil," she said, and Sarah realized that "home" had meant Felicity's pad.

On the thirty-fourth floor of a block near Lincoln Center, the apartment was decorated solely by the view. Sarah was mesmerized. From the river on one side to the lights of Central Park South on the other, the canyons of the city unfolded to the gaze. "If I lived here I'd do nothing but stare," said Sarah. She turned around. Felicity had gone. There was nothing in the room except cushions and bean bags on the floor, a rug and a poster or two. Plants trailed from a rack near the ceiling and the last we'll hear of John Lennon was relayed through five stereo speakers carefully positioned around the place. The smell of an incense candle wafted in from somewhere but the lights of the city outside, were the only light in the room.

Sarah wandered into the bedroom where Felicity was undressing slowly by the incense candle's glow, watching herself with pleasure in a long mirror. She beckoned Sarah to a seat on the huge bed which occupied the floor. She was quite absorbed in her own performance, smiling beguilingly at herself as her tights came off and then her bra. She massaged her breasts and the nipples stood up, then she took off her pants and rubbed her curly pubic hair. Last of all she took down the mass of curls pinned to the top of her head and shook them so her hair was free. It fell almost to her waist.

"You've got a gorgeous figure," Sarah said, amused. "No wonder you're proud of it. Do you diet?"

"Oh, not really. But I only eat raw food. I haven't had anything cooked for at least three years. Feel my breasts. See how firm they are? You can't keep that up on gourmet food, you know. Do you want to fuck?"

Felicity curled up on the bed and put her head on Sarah's lap. She was like a child, or a childish cat, and Sarah stroked her hair. "No, I don't," she said. "I think you're lovely and I've nothing against doing it with women. So far I've never wanted to. And I think you should only fuck when you really want to. I try to stick to that."

"No sweat," said Felicity, contented as any cat. "You don't have to explain. Would you like some herbal tea?"

They sat in the semi-darkness for a while, listening to the words of "Starting Over" and "Woman, I owe Everything to You" and sharing a joint.

"This mattress is like a raft up here in the sky," Sarah said. "We could float out of the window on it and be among the stars and the skyscrapers."

"Everyone lives on rafts in New York City," Felicity said. "Rafts moored insecurely in mid-air and surrounded by loneliness. They bump into skyscrapers sometimes, but they never bump into one another."

"Air traffic control must be keen."

"We're isolated," Felicity sighed. "And we say all we want is space."

They called Sarah a cab and she fell into bed in her shabby mid-town room and slept.

Next day she went down to Greenwich Village to visit the

Emerging offices. Gerry, the celibate editor, seemed cross with her. Huge photos of the elect stared down at her from the walls – Margaret Mead, Louise Nevelson. She wondered what she had done. Apparently some of her ladies were not fast enough, while others were too fast. And all of them had cared too much for men. Sarah herself had hedged her attitudes. "Your pieces are not politicized," said Gerry, shaking her braless bosom loweringly.

"No," said Sarah politely, trying to fathom this.

"Then neither are you," threatened Gerry.

She went to see her friend Diana at a publishing house in a vast mid-town Manhattan building. Diana's offices were on the nineteenth floor. On the ninth floor a man who looked like a figure from a New Yorker cartoon of the fifties, square cut raincoat, belted, cowlick of hair, got into the elevator and spied a man he recognized in the corner. "Oh, Mr Gee," he said. "I have something to tell you. My mother liked your book." There seemed to be a special emphasis on the word "mother", a special venom. As pronounced by this man in this elevator the word "mother" was meaningful, it was significant. It held the kind of significance the word "mother" can hold in no other town. "Now that's the good news," the man continued, as the elevator elevated them to the fifteenth floor. "The bad news is" he paused, "my *mother*–" his tongue curled round the poisoned word possessively, "my *mother* has just been committed." The doors opened on the eighteenth floor and the man with the mother got out without a backward glance. The mouth of the man to whom these remarks had been addressed had also opened, but alas, the nineteenth floor arrived, so Sarah would never know if he would ever get it shut again.

She and Diana were pleased to see each other. They hugged and their smiles seemed hooked around their ears to stay. They went down in the elevator. It filled with kids going out to lunch. A boy looked at a girl across the crowd. "What do you wanna eat?" he asked, as the lift rushed down. "I don't care," said the girl, moodily, "as long as it isn't hamburger." The boy considered this through thirteen floors, chewing gum the while. Finally he looked at her again, one eyebrow up. "You wanna eat ethnic?" he asked her.

Diana hailed a taxi and they went down and across and down again and got out by a battered playground bounded by broken wire netting in one of those streets which seem all blue and red and grey and yellow and black. It may be that trees are planted in these streets. It may be that trees grow, but if so, they do not add the colour green to these sidewalks. The colours here are urban colours, and the smell is metal, tough.

Sarah followed Diana through passageways, empty gyms, a couple of dusty classrooms, till they found the place. Trampolines lined the floor and there were bars and a "horse" or two. Diana's nine-year-old daughter, Daisy, was doing gym. The two women sat down on chairs and endeavoured to talk, while Daisy went through her paces sturdily. She arched her small back, pointed her toes, did pirouettes, handstands, somersaults. She jumped, leapfrogged, swung. She willed them to watch her, to stop their stupid chatter and to pay attention. She wanted them to see that, alone among all the other prancing nine-year olds, she was Daisy. And one day she'd be somebody. She would be herself. Outside, under pitiless clear skies the hard-edged city, the city Daisy would inherit, fought through another day. "Wait for me!

Wait for me!" said the arches of her arms as they stretched farther upward. Upward. Daisy, emerging.

Alone once more, Sarah struggled through a throng of black girl students outside Carnegie Hall. In starched graduate gowns and pristine mortar boards, they vied with each other to have their photos taken by parents, in this, their finest hour, the end of another school year. Emotions ran high: parents kissed daughters, students kissed everyone in sight, tears of joy were shed, cries of congratulation filled the air. Pushing her way through this happy crowd, Sarah felt quite churned up herself. Young America, the brave and the free. Were not these students all our futures? But all this emotion at the end of each school year? That was the thing about this city: everyone tried so hard. "How do you get to Carnegie Hall?" a student asks an old lady in the well known New York joke, and gets a shrug, an admonition for an answer.

"Practice!"

That's how you get to Carnegie Hall.

ENCOUNTERS/ENCOUNTERS

It is over half a century since Anita Loos loosed the blonde gentlemen prefer on an avid world. Maybe things haven't changed as much as we think they have in that time after all. Of course, a girl gets older and is bound to lose some of her assets on the way, but neither Lorelei Lee nor her diminutive creator seem to have lost their freshness, their appeal, their *jwa de veevra.* Anita still lives in her comfortable New York apartment opposite Carnegie Hall and life is still pretty well wrinkle free as she ironed it in that first fine careless edition of 1925. She still has her cute dark bangs and her disbelieving laugh. Diamonds still sparkle in the snazzy winged frames of her spectacles. She still gets photographed in the glossies wearing skin-tight leopard trousers and a cigarette holder whilst lounging against gold lamé cushions. She's still writing. She's still a success. And gentlemen still prefer blondes.

Before she was thirty, Anita had retired from Hollywood. She had written over 200 film scripts and thought it enough. "I quit work because I had made so much money. In those days all Americans were rich. We all gambled on the stock market and it was a bullish stock-market. You could take a thousand dollars and wind it up into a million in six weeks. Besides, I hated Hollywood. Always did. And, of course, you could go anywhere in Europe. It was lazing in the resorts of the world which drove me to write *Blondes*. I got so bored with all that Riviera life. And then I got even richer . . .

"I wrote the first chapter as a joke. I never thought of it as a book at all. But H. L. Mencken was a *mash* of mine. I was really *mashed* on him, and he was having a – playing with a blonde, and I said: 'I'll fix her.' So I wrote her up."

When Anita Loos is consumed with laughter, it is best to wait until that laughter subsides.

"Did it fix her?" I asked, eventually.

"As a matter of fact, it did, because by the time it appeared he had ten other blondes."

Another pause for laughter.

"I never thought of it as a book. I wrote it on a train going to Hollywood. I was going there on a job and I put it in a suitcase and forgot all about it, and when I came back to New York and was unpacking, I ran into it, and I sent it to Mencken as a joke, never thinking of it being published. But he called me up from Baltimore, and he said: I've read this, and it should be published. I'd publish it in the *Mercury* (which he'd just started) but I have to be careful. And he said: You know you're the first American ever to make fun of sex."

Anita laughs as if she'd never believed any of this, and isn't going to start now.

"He said: Send it to *Harpers Bazaar*, which is a women's fashion magazine, and it will get lost in the ads and won't shock anybody. So I sent it to *Harpers Bazaar* and the editor there – an old boy – I call him old, but he couldn't have been old then, he only died this year – sent for me and said: 'This is okay and I'm going to publish it, but,' he said, 'why do you stop? You've started a girl for Europe. Why don't you take her on her trip?' Well, I was leaving for Europe myself, so I said all right, and he said get me in a second instalment, and send one in for each month of *Harpers Bazaar*, which I did."

"It was such a success that by the third issue the news-stand sales had multiplied by ten. Men's goods like cigars started to be advertised in *Harpers Bazaar*.

"Was that because of the 'Gentlemen' of the title?"

"No. Just because the sales were so big. The magazine became the biggest selling magazine in America."

"So you were the magic lady who put the circulation up."

"Yes," she said, disbelievingly. "I really put that thing on the map. It was only after this enormous success in *Harpers Bazaar* that the book was brought out. I had a Beau who was at Liveright (the publishers) and he was Horace Liveright's assistant, and he said to me, 'why don't I get out some copies of *Gentlemen Prefer Blondes* for you to give away at Christmas as Christmas presents?' He said, 'there's no use making an issue of it because it's for a very small limited public, and they've all read it in the magazine, but it would be nice if you had these copies,' and he got out twenty-five hundred of them. They were the first edition. They were gone the morning they landed in the book-shops. And the second edition was sixty-five thousand.

"I never had a pleasant moment after that. I couldn't enjoy a thing. My husband was so jealous of me, made me so miserable that I didn't want to write. I didn't want to write anything. And a doctor had told me, a psychologist, he said, 'Your husband's going to lose his mind unless you quit writing,' and I didn't mind giving it up. It meant nothing to me. So I quit. But the following year the editor of *Harpers* begged me to write *Gentlemen Marry Brunettes*, and I wrote it in terrible circumstances."

There is a very interesting dedication to *Brunettes*. It reads as follows:

To John Emerson, who discovered, developed,
fostered and trained whatever I may have, if I
have anything, that is worth while.

It availed her nothing. As Mencken wrote: A husband may survive the fact of a wife *having* more money than he, but if she earns more, it can destroy his very essence.

"At that time, I was still in love with John and trying to be a nursemaid and trying to look out for him and pampering him, which he adored, and at the same time I was driving him nuts. No wonder the man landed in a sanitarium."

"Was he a writer, your husband?"

"No. He just – he did what Colette's husband did, really. He put his name on everything I wrote – 'by John Emerson and Anita Loos.'"

"What, on all those two hundred scripts?"

"Well, the first two hundred or so, I

was only a child, but as soon as I met him – he was a director in Hollywood when we met and had been an important Broadway director before that, he was twenty years older than me – as soon as I met him he started putting my scripts on film and then they became by John Emerson . . ."

"But when you published *Gentlemen Prefer Blondes* it was under your name alone?"

"Yes. He didn't want any part of that. He didn't think it was worth anything."

"And then it became a success . . ."

"Yes." A quiet kind of laugh. "He blew it wrong."

"Did it ruin the marriage in the end?"

For the first and only time that afternoon, Anita's voice changed down into the minor key.

"It sent him into a sanitarium for eighteen years," she said, holding the note for a beat or so on that "eighteen years".

Then her laugh moved into major and we were off again.

"Did you feel guilty about it?"

"No. I was having too good a time. And nothing could have saved him. He just became an ultra hypochondriac with so many diseases based on . . ."

"His response to your success."

"Men are so – I feel sorry for men because they're so sensitive. They really are eaten up with sensibilities. And they have no real accomplishments in themselves."

"So they take achievement much more seriously?"

"Yes. But the men that I cared for after my husband didn't give a damn about it. And I very soon lost all interest in my marriage. I kept it going because I was paying all the bills and looking out for him, but the men I had great fun with didn't give a damn about it. In fact they liked the fact that you were a success. They didn't even consider it. They didn't any more consider it than I did. Of course, none of them were immediately competitive with me in the way John was. What were they? Well, for a while in England there was Viscount D'Abernon. Then, one of them was what we call a con man. Another was a gag writer at MGM. And then there was H. L. Mencken, who I always adored till one day he died, and who really – he would take on these blondes, one after the other, but it never affected our relationship because there was nothing sexy about it. It was just fond."

It appears that, after the devastating

collapse of her marriage, Anita's love affairs stopped short of consummation and/or marriage. Men were pals, and she had the greatest fun with them, but she couldn't trust them enough for total commitment. Put it another way. She chose characters who for one reason or another, were unable to commit themselves totally to her.

Anita's rooms are studded with glowing paintings: Anita by Rouault, a Picasso or two, and over by the window in the light, a beautiful Jack B. Yeats in which a pretty blonde stands by a bookstall in the street watching a man browse through the books. The title of this painting: Gentlemen Prefer Books.

It is difficult to imagine any book published today having the kind of success Anita Loos had with *Gentlemen Prefer Blondes*. People in every corner of the globe went bananas for it. James Joyce saved his failing eyesight to read it; the Chinese translated Lorelei's jargon into the vernacular of the Sing Sing girls; it was called "the best book of philosophy written by an American" by George Santayana who was an American philosopher; it was called "*the* great American novel", by Edith Wharton, herself a great American novelist. Following in her heroine's footsteps, Anita created a sensation wherever she went, even Bedford Square. Lytton Strachey referred to her as "the divine A." in a letter to Lady Ottoline Morrell, and Cecil Beaton described her as "the quintessence of cuteness". You can see from the photographs they do not exaggerate.

Her study is crowded with books and photos inscribed to her by the folk heroes of our times: To Anita. To Nita. To Neetsie. To Bugs and to Buggie. From Ernest, Scott, Christopher, Aldous. Jean Harlow, Carole Lombard, Greta Garbo, Audrey Hepburn, Douglas Fairbanks, Clark Gable, Fred and Adele Astaire, Irving Thalberg and Norma Shearer, Paulette Goddard et al. Intimates all, and for a lot of the time she knew them, Anita was the one who was famous. William Empson wrote a poem entitled "Reflection from Anita Loos" in which the refrain goes "A girl can't go on laughing all the time," a phrase he said Anita had said to him, though Anita herself cannot remember saying it. On the last birthday of his life, Scott Fitzgerald acknowledged her fame in her autograph book:

This book tells that Anita Loos
Is a friend of Caesar, a friend of Zeus,

Of Samuel Goldwyn, and Mother Goose,
Of Balanchine of the Ballet Russe,
Of Tillie the Viennese papoose
Of Charlie MacArthur on the loose
Of Shanks, chiropodists – what's the use?
Of actors who have escaped the noose
Lots of Hollywood beach refuse
Comics covered with Charlotte Russe
Wretched victims of self-abuse
Big producers, all obtuse
This is my birthday, but what the deuce
Is that sad fact to Anita Loos.

"Scott had the most idiotic ambition. He wanted to be a film writer, and nothing could have been more silly because he was at the very top of the heap doing the thing he did well. And it killed him, really, that his films were no good. And writing films is just a knack. It isn't even a talent. It's just a knack. The best films we did at MGM were written by a woman who couldn't write two sentences, but she could sit in a conference and spin out stories. She was a plot expert. Zelda? Oh, Zelda was a danger to be with. A compulsive stripper in public who thought her body was delectable. There wasn't much to flaunt. Talullah Bankhead used to strip off whenever she had the chance and she didn't have much either, but she got away with it through an impish desire to shock. But Zelda was the biggest bore. Such a crasher that if I saw her coming I jumped out of the way."

Gladys, a generous black lady from the south who had taken care of Anita now for many years brings us a fresh pot of palest tea. She gives Anita her post, her messages, pats her on the shoulder, beams at me. Warmth flows between two women who have lived their lives together. What's in the post? News of another musical, with Carol Channing as Lorelei. A possible new film. The galleys of a piece for – *Harpers Bazaar. Plus ça change*... Anita pours the tea. The laugh still purring under her breath makes her hand a bit unsteady but she manages. William Empson was clearly wrong. A girl can go on laughing all the time. It's a pleased kind of laugh. A brunette laugh. And the purr is a brunette purr. Blondes never purr. For what can you do but laugh when you've been dealt such cards? All life must be a joke. Well, mustn't it? Anita Loos is pleased. Not with life, or herself, but with the cards dealt her.

12

Tiredness and the queasiness that follows the eating of plastic, warmed-up food at an altitude of 30,000 feet and trying to sleep sitting up after you've eaten it, gave way to relief as Sarah sped towards Central London. Her London! The greenness, the human scale of it! Familiarity. Thank goodness she didn't cross the river on this route; she'd probably cry. From the flyover she saw into streets and crescents of eccentric houses, pebble-dash, grey brick, purple brick, yellow brick with white stone facings, stucco in varying stages of repair; pride to decay. How strange to feel she knew things about the people in these houses, odd intimate things, like the furniture they lived with, their style in lampshades, the position of the television set in their living room. She could even make an informed guess at the books in their meagre bookshelves, the magazines and newspapers in their racks, the medicines in their bathroom cabinets. She knew the jars and bottles on each woman's dressing table and the jams and spices in each different kitchen. She saw the women, pottering about after dinner, muttering to themselves: "tomorrow I will do something with my life!" How lucky she was to have a job, Sarah thought. To be part of the hub of this metropolis. Oh, half the time working was sheer frustration it was true, but however hellish, how lucky to be one of the few women who had the chance to work, the chance to show that women are not only as good as, though different from, men but, sometimes even better. At every party, there was a woman who came up and said to Sarah, "Oh, I long to work, like you, but what could I do?" Or worse: "Oh, women's magazines. Yes, I've always meant to write one of those stories, if only I could find the time."

David had stayed up to welcome her, and had amended the front door "Welcome Home" notice he had painted for Adam's last return, the letters for "Mummy" being unevenly stuck over "Daddy" and the lions and tigers of Africa uneasily transformed into skyscrapers. Prevailed upon, eventually, to go to bed, he insisted on wearing the new Chinese pyjamas Sarah had brought him, and clutching a toy guitar in one hand and a Big Apple mug in the other.

"Gosh, it's nice to be home," Sarah sighed, reclining at last on the sofa, shoes off, drink in hand.

"Well, don't settle in," Adam warned her. "We're going to Hollywood."

Sarah sat up so suddenly she spilt her drink. "We're *what*?"

"I've had an offer," he grinned. "Don't laugh, baby. This is for real. It's the offer of a lifetime. One of the big studios is starting a documentary department. They've been over here and asked me to head it for them. Set it up. There are millions of dollars at stake. They want me to go there for a few days soon to get the feel of it."

"And you've accepted? Without even checking with me?"

"But, honey . . ."

"Don't 'honey' me, we're not in L. A. yet. This is my life, as well as yours, not to mention David's. All that trouble we went to, choosing schools."

"He can commute. I've thought it through, Sarah. Winchester terms. Hols in Topanga Canyon. He'll love it. So would I have done. He's a lucky kid."

"It's not as easy as that, Adam. It's years before he goes to Winchester. I wouldn't leave him here at Prep School with us on the other side of the world."

"He can go to school there, then."

"That means American Education all the way through till Oxford." She paused. "And what about me? My job, my friends?"

"Oh, love, you can write anywhere. That's the beauty of it. You can interview ancient film stars."

"Thanks."

She knew what it would be like: she'd be stranded on Malibu Beach, at the edge of the world. She'd be Mrs Adam Cornish, not Sarah. She'd be an appendage again. She'd be lost.

'Whither thou goest, I will go," she muttered later, sliding, sleepless, out of bed without disturbing the even rumble of Adam's snoring. She crept into the kitchen and warmed some milk with a spoonful of honey. Cradling the mug in her hands she stared out of her window at her view. Her London, the centre of her world.

No kids played in Mel's front garden, and the welcoming open door was shut. Strange. No shrieks of joy or rage assailed Sarah's ears. No noise. She pressed the bell. It didn't work. She remembered, now, it never had. She rattled the letter box, and banged.

Eventually, a white-faced Mel opened the door, said "Oh!" and flung herself heavily into Sarah's arms. Staggering slightly, Sarah asked, "What's wrong?"

"Can't tell you here," sniffed Mel. "Come through."

In the sitting room the children sat round the walls in silence, colouring on their knees, their tongues between their teeth. David, absorbed, was playing noughts and crosses in indelible purple pentel on his and the next boy's legs. He looked up and mouthed a silent "I'm winning" at her.

"You must have sellotaped their tongues."

"Not quite."

"What happened?"

Removing a cardboard crate or two, Mel shut the kitchen door. "They tried to fire me. They want to close me down. I'm not fit to be a baby minder, they said." She began to cry. "Oh, they're right, you know. That's the trouble. I broke all the rules, I crammed too many kids in, I let them run wild. There was even evidence that drink was consumed on the premises during nursery hours. Your actual alcohol!" She brightened for a moment. "Would you like some?"

"Have you got any juice?" asked Sarah.

Mel poured them both orange juice and sat down again, wearily.

"This is the only job I'm good at. What on earth will I do instead?"

Sarah glared at her. "You are wet. You can't give in! I

won't let you! We'll put on a fight. Challenge them. We'll win. You'll see. We'll get Adam's help."

"The full weight of Television. That should fix 'em." For a moment, Mel beamed. "The kids *love* me," she said. And then she was howling again. "The children are happy here. That's what they can't stand. Or understand. That's what gets their goat. And I love doing it," she wailed. "It makes me happy."

"Adam wants us to move to Hollywood."

Mel stopped wailing instantly.

"Good God," she said. "He can't. I mean, you can't. You'll go bananas. And so will I. This calls for stronger things." She unearthed a bottle of Bell's from the sideboard.

"It's funny," mused Sarah. "I've been having a horrid time. The two mothers, and all this death and problems at work. Sometimes, just recently, I've longed to escape, to run away. But not to Malibu." She shivered. "The edge of the world. I dreamed last night that I'd fallen off, and was clinging to rocks and the edges of cliffs. But the rocks are all made of celluloid, there, you know, so I couldn't get a grip."

Mel chuckled. "Yes. Very little grasp on reality. I've heard. If you want to run away, we can go to France, as we've always planned. I've seen just the house for us. We can sit in the sun. There's an orchard. And poppies and long grass. A verandah. Needs fixing, of course, and so does the roof. We can grow things and drink wine and get fat and have fun. We don't have to wait till we're old . . ."

"I thought you said that when we're old, our famous country house home will have to be in town."

"Well, it's nearer for hospitals and shops and welfare and things."

"It's not the same," grumbled Sarah. "I can't dream about that. It was all those home grown vegetables and herbs from our walled kitchen garden we were going to put in the soup."

"Wherever it is, we'll make soup and look after each other and any surviving friends."

"Or lovers."

"Those too. Those, too."

"I met a girl in the office today," Sarah said. "She's got everything you're supposed to have, you know, husband, and children and job and nice house and money. She was looking a bit desperate, I thought, a bit haggard, she'd got what we on the problem page call 'the young wives under stress look'. It's unmistakable. And this girl said to me: 'You know, Sarah, I used to think there were only two real luxuries in life, sex and pure silk. Now I know there's only one, and it's being alone . . .'"

"It is pretty weird, I suppose," said Mel. "There are all these young women longing for time alone in which to discover themselves. Refusing marriage, or deliberately breaking marriages up to get some space around them. To get their acts together. And all these older women living alone at the end of their lives, lonely as hell, and hating it."

Adam grabbed David's legs from among the toys and bubbles in the bath and scrubbed them none too gently with the loofah.

"I told you," said David triumphantly. "It won't come off!"

He examined the uneven purple patches of noughts and crosses with pride. Adam caught Sarah's eyes across his head.

"I can't think why you want to preserve all this," said Adam. "It's not exactly pretty."

"I won," said David scornfully.

His parents looked at him with disapproval.

"I see," said Sarah.

"We have bred a competitive son," said Adam.

"Did you want me to lose?" challenged David.

How easily Adam had grown into a father, thought Sarah, as she watched him carry David pick-a-back to bed. With what ease and assurance he played the rôle, and what confidence it seemed to have brought to other areas of his life. He was so much more relaxed. After all her fears, having a child had brought them closer together. It was amazing luck to discover, or re-discover after all these years how much she *liked* the man she was married to. In marriages there was always love and hate in widely differing proportions, but very rarely liking. Like the loving kindness spoken of in prayers, it seemed an old-fashioned kind of virtue. In all Sarah's unusually varied friendships, there were few women who had stayed married to the husbands they'd met when so bitterly young and green, and even fewer who had stayed with the man because they *liked* him.

"You must have known she'd get the boot," Adam said over dinner. "You know your Mel."

"But it's so unfair. The children *love* her. They're happy there."

"Look, she's Unconventional," said Adam patiently. "We're dealing with the Council."

Sarah sighed. "It's the old chestnut, all right. Humanity

versus Bureaucracy. Love against the State. Warmth versus Rules . . ."

"Oh God."

"Will you help?"

"I suppose so," said Adam, gloomily.

Sarah watched as Adela picked out coloured wools in a tapestry shop. She certainly had an eye, and seemed immensely sure of the subtleties. An earnest discussion with the assistant ensued about the thicknesses of different wools and the size of the holes in various canvases.

"You mustn't have them too small," warned Sarah. "You'll strain your eyes."

"And then I'll blame you, since this was all your idea."

One of my better ones, thought Sarah. Adela seemed quite excited at the prospect of doing something, though she remained dubious about whether she could do it well. She bought skeins of dusty pink and forest green and forget-me-not blue to the window for Sarah's inspection, and Sarah thought suddenly of the time she herself had been taught to knit, aged six, a six-stitch scarf, as she remembered, for her teddy bear. They were deep in the country somewhere and she had been taken to a village shop where a kindly woman had produced a cardboard box of penny balls of wool. They had glowed at Sarah out of the dark interior of that shop, as fresh and enticing as still wet paint, or freshly licked lollipops, bright yellow and orange and emerald green. Bright purple and brilliant blue. She had stared at them enchanted, but she knew from the beginning which one she had to have. A very shocking pink. It was the brightest of them all.

They repaired to a coffee shop.

"You know, I could paint the designs myself, on plain canvas," Adela said. "I used to be able to paint."

"Now *that* would be something," said Sarah. "Really original designs. You could make all sorts of things."

"You could design them and I could make them," Adela said.

"Handbags and carpet bags and waistcoats, as well as cushions and pictures and wall hangings. You'd get commissioned."

"I couldn't do it quickly enough for that." Adela patted Sarah's hands across the table. "How you encourage me," she said. "I think I will take up painting again. I liked it so much when I was young. There are classes, you know, at the Institute. Maybe I should go?"

Sarah allowed herself a sigh of relief and ordered a piece of apple strudel with her coffee. Was it possible that Adela could stand on her own feet after all, that she would make some kind of tentative life for herself, after all these years?

"I was considered talented when I was a girl, you know. Before I married. I was not as clever as my friend Moushka. She was always top of the class. But I was more talented. More artistic."

Adela's face, as she talked of these things, became younger and younger. Her voice and her mannerisms grew girlish and eager. She sat up straight in her chair with her chin up and the faded blue eyes seemed deep with mischief. She smiled. An independent person sat before Sarah, a person with promise. The kind of person you could imagine getting on the local train from Cracow to Wieliczka. Aged twenty and fashionably dressed, her long blonde hair elaborately drawn into a bun like a cottage loaf, selecting a carriage, selecting a window seat, settling down. In the opposite corner of the carriage, a boy with the long silk coat, big hat and long side curls of the Orthodox Jews sat quietly, only the stillness of his long, pale face betraying fear. Facing him sat two rough Polish boys, elbows on knees, flick knives pointing steadily at his eyes.

"Stop frightening that poor boy!" said the girl, commandingly.

Without a word, the louts got up and left.

The young Adela had beauty and she knew it. She had talent and she knew it. She had confidence and pride. "I can conquer the world," her look said. "I am Adela. I am me. But first, I suppose I should get married."

"The most brilliant needlewoman, of course, was my mother. She did tapestries, embroidered linen, open-work table cloths, even lace. There's a piece of lace curtaining she made with a shepherd and shepherdess on it . . . You've seen it, Sarah."

"You don't often talk about her, do you?"

"I suppose I'm always talking about my father. I was so much in love with him that when he was away – he travelled a lot across Europe buying and selling forests, you know – I didn't sleep."

"I bet your mother took a dim view of that."

"I learned to disguise my sleepless nights from her. My mother was never interested in sex. She never once enjoyed it. She used to tell me herself she didn't know how she'd had five children. She just lay there, she said, and he 'did his job', and she hated it. It was the worst thing she had to do. I think my father was a sexy man who loved and desired his wife and wanted her to react to him. It must have been a great puzzle to him. She was so feminine in every other way and she bore his children easily. He was a confident man, and never had any doubts that he, himself, was physically and sexually attractive. He took her to Berlin once to consult a doctor about it and the doctor told her that she was sexually dead but that she should drink champagne. So from then on my father ordered champagne and she drank it, but it didn't help.

"The funny thing is that after I'd been married for about three years and we were living in Germany, I took *my* husband to the doctor. I wanted a baby. I had not conceived. Alas, the doctor did not prescribe champagne. He simply told us it was nerves. Nerves! Bah! I should have left Jacob. I know I should have done." Adela sighed. "The trouble was that somewhere along the way, I'd fallen in love with him."

"Fallen in love." The fatal words echoed in Sarah's mind like the words of a hundred songs.

"Well, I must have done. My father visited us a second time in Dusseldorf and again I knew this was my chance. Escape! Poor father. He admired our new acquisitions: such modern Bauhaus furniture we had, and the English Silver, and the portrait of me, tight-lipped, which Jacob had commissioned. He went along our street tapping the linden trees – he never could pass a tree without telling you its state of health. But it was after the shock, you see, his own men turned against him and hunted him with pitch-forks, you remember. He was never the same again. Oh, there he sat, loving and kind and beautifully dressed as ever, witty and wise and warm. But he was not my father as I want to remember him. He was a tremulous old man. How could I give this man another shock, or add my problems to his own?

"Besides, by this time, Jacob's coldness had become a challenge to me. Could I get him to react? I tried everything: temperament and tears, babyish pouts and sulks and cool, grown-up disdain. I fed him liver and oysters and caviar. Gave him my breasts to suck. Provoked. Deferred. Nothing changed. I tried again. I was remorseless. I never gave up, you know. Not till a year before the end. Years later he told me he would have liked to commit suicide on our wedding night. Well, maybe it was my fault, too. I was like a block of wood. So virginal. So stupid. I'd never been kissed, never been touched by man. Everything was sleeping in me. I just lay there, waiting.

"I went back to that doctor once, in Germany, the one who had mentioned nerves. He was nice and good looking and kind, and I could see that he liked me. You can always tell. He had me strapped up with my legs spread wide on one of those high tables they have with lights, and he started to examine me and I thought 'this is your chance, I could get pregnant here and no one would ever know'. I watched him lean over me and his face came closer and my arms got ready to go around his neck. I can still remember it: his face coming down towards me for a kiss. And I couldn't do it. At the last moment I pushed his head away. He knew how close it had been. He could hear my heart."

Adela stared over Sarah's head into the past and her clear blue eyes grew wistful.

"I should have had lots of children," she said, "then I should not have had to swamp my poor little only child with love. To threaten. To overwhelm . . ." She brought her gaze back to Sarah and added persuasively: "He does not seem to have suffered too much from it, does he? He hasn't developed a don't-touch-me attitude because I tried to kiss and cuddle him too much?"

Sarah lowered her eyes and felt a blush spreading across her face and neck. "It was a good thing, after all, that he married you so young," Adela continued. "Before my possessiveness and over-protectiveness could damage him." She paused. "No, Adam's a warm, affectionate boy, thank God. He's like me. He hasn't inherited the remoteness of his father."

13

ENCOUNTERS/ENCOUNTERS

I remember Ivy standing by the creeper of the same name, outside the house in Hove. She was waving goodbye to us, her lovely smile, white, even-toothed, revealing suddenly the girl she had been. She was eighty-five years young, vigorous, opinionated, talkative as ever. Her brilliant white hair, thick and springy, attracted light, so that all her quicksilver changes of expression (so Gemini!) seemed illuminated by it. Her voice needed no such emphasis: swooping and pouncing in glee or malice, laughing or enunciating carefully so we should not miss her meaning, her voice held all the assurance of her Bloomsbury background. She stood by the ivy-covered wall, an old woman wearing a man's black trousers, and a man's striped shirt, and she seemed to combine in her body, the strength of the men she had known with the charm of the woman she had been.

It had been an extraordinary afternoon. Ivy served us lunch. There were three guests, and we sat, very properly, around a card table set up in the passageway of her ground floor flat. The table had been carefully laid. The napkins were paper serviettes of the thin, pre-Kleenex kind, and each had been torn in two. Flushed with her culinary problems, Ivy appeared in the doorway brandishing the grill. "Now, how do you like your steaks?" she asked. "Medium? Rare? Well done?" We described how we liked our steaks, and much clattering went on off stage. Eventually a piece of steak arrived, thin, overdone and curling disdainfully round the edges. With a gaiety the Russians must have envied, Ivy approached it with a carving knife. "Now, how shall I cut it in four?" she mused.

I had first gone to see Ivy with a friend who shared the same surname as her famous diplomat husband, Maxim Litvinov. They were not related but had swapped stories about people and ideas and things Russian in an animated way. The people and ideas interested Ivy. Things Russian did not. It might even be true to say that during her stay in the country she had married into, a stay which lasted almost all her adult life, little of its strangeness or barbarity had impinged upon her. A Cambridge and Bloomsbury child, daughter of a linguist father and a novelist mother, Ivy took her own fringed-lampshade world with her to Moscow, and sat always under the familiar comfort of its glow, re-reading Jane Austen, while sipping Russian tea.

She's a great Janeite. For years she's longed to write an article about Jane Austen in Russia. "It's a lovely idea, but now it's too late. The whole of the first decade I was in Russia I had writer's block. I resorted in the end, to a hypnotist. Eventually, I produced a detective story, *His Master's Voice*, first published in 1930. Later on, I wrote long short stories and they were published during the sixties in the *New Yorker*, but during the whole of my young married life I was trying and trying to write a proper novel."

There could be no excuses! She had time and space in the large old-fashioned rooms they had settled in opposite the domes of the Kremlin, her children were in kindergarten, Maxim was a dear. And it wasn't, after all, as if she were taking the plunge. As "little Ivy Low" she had had two successful novels to her name before the war, the first world war, she says in emphasis. "Before I met my husband. Before I was married. The first was *Growing Pains* and people were kind about it, very kind."

"What was it like?"

"Oh, it was mystical," said Ivy vaguely, in the most precise of voices. "And commonplace. It wasn't read by many, but Mudie's took it up and that was good. You couldn't get anywhere without Mudie's in those days. Do you remember Mudie's?"

"Well . . . Not quite . . ."

"Oh, I couldn't im*a*gine life without Mudie's," Ivy says, drawing the "a" in "imagine" to exaggerated lengths. "It was the original lending library in Oxford Street where fashionable people borrowed novels. I was *banned* by Mudie's. Then one day I came back from Russia and it was gone . . . They banned my second book, *The Questing Beast.*" Her voice holds pride and challenge in it still. And why? It contained these lines:

Said Girl to Man: What'll I do if I have a baby?

Said Man to Girl: Don't worry. I'll take care of all that.

"There was a marvellous woman, a columnist who was writing for the *Daily Mirror*, an American, and she went into Mudie's – they knew her there – and she must have read the book – it had been reviewed – and she said 'I want *The Questing Beast* by Ivy Low.' 'Sorry Madam', they said," and here, Ivy's voice dropped to the merest whisper, "'we can't let you have *that* over the counter'."

"Just that day there were piles and piles and piles of Elinor Glyn – you know, *Three Weeks* – you wouldn't call her pornographic, would you? Sort of, cheap erotica – and this woman said, aren't you ashamed of yourselves. Here's all this tripe, and here's a young gel trying to tell the truth."

"Your mother was a novelist, too, wasn't she? What did she say when you published your first novel?"

"Nothing encouraging."

"Was she any good? What was her name?"

"Oh, you've never heard of her. Alice Herbert. A bright, upper class kind of lady, like – you know – Ada Leverson, the one who befriended Oscar Wilde. She was witty. And she wasted *all* her substance. She reviewed and reviewed and reviewed..."

"Were you close to your mother?"

"Close. And then a beast."

"And then a beast? Who was a beast? You?"

"Yes."

"Why?"

Ivy paused then, and directed a piercing gaze at me.

"Well," she said, enunciating extra clearly, "Have you a mother?"

I gulped, and said I had, and that I, too, was a beast.

"My father died when I was five, you see. My mother was thirty, then. She married again within the year. Who to? Oh, a nasty bore. A nasty little bore. I've got it all written down." She laughed victoriously. "It's all in my stories, *She Knew She was Right.*

"My mother ruined us with all that early sex talk. Even when I was very small she implicated me in her affairs. I was a sort of accessory, I suppose, whenever she could see that a small girl might make a pretty contrast to her seductive self. You shouldn't do that sort of thing to children. It ruins them. I was careful as anything with my daughter. I did things differently. Then, later, at sixteen, when I came home from boarding school, my mother made a confidante of me, an absolute confidante. She told me about all her affairs and everything, forced me into things I wasn't ready for and didn't really want. Older people simply loathed me. She was a siren, my mother. An absolute siren. I used to repeat every word she said.

"When I was with the Lawrences, Frieda Lawrence behaved like that: she just came out with everything Lawrence had said before. I got to know Lawrence through the TLS. They ran a series declaring they'd found the ten most promising new writers. None of them were any good except Lawrence, so I wrote and told them so. I stayed with the Lawrences in Fiascherino, near Lerici in Italy. Lawrence would put his head out of the window when he was writing *Women in Love* and say 'Girls, what colour stockings shall she wear?' And we'd look at our legs and say 'green', and green they'd be. We were literary influences, you see.

"I fled from my mother, from home, and from stuffy academia, too, the moment I could. I got my odd little room on the heights of Hampstead. Lovely! It was like running away to live in an attic in Montmartre. It was marvellous in Hampstead. You could hear Katherine Mansfield and John Middleton Murry quarrelling from your back garden. And that was where I met Maxim. A typing agency had sent me to him, and I spent the first hours of our relationship typing his letters about agricultural affairs. Some of our meeting is described in my story *Call it Love*."

They were married in February 1917 at Hampstead Town Hall and went to Russia in time for the Revolution. When they returned, Maxim Litvinov was representing the new Bolshevik government in London, and was later to become its Ambassador here. It is probable, however, that it is for the impact he made as Minister at the time of the League of Nations, and for his remark "Peace is indivisible" that he is best remembered.

"But I want to tell you about my sister," said Ivy. "I had a fascinating sister. She wasn't nearly so close to my mother as I was. She was one year and three days younger than me. I wasn't a very popular girl – I think I was scared – but she was madly popular, a wild organizer of clubs and dances and God knows what. She was so popular with boys and girls in every way, and do you know how it all turned out? All her boyfriends married her girlfriends, and I don't think she ever understood why."

"Why were you scared? Because you were clever?"

"Because I was neither flesh nor fish... Because of my mother. It was very complicated. I mean I think I was made artificially into a kind of sexy person, but I think I was really very puritanical and it spoiled everything because the boys all thought 'Here's an intelligent girl behaving like a vamp. What does she want?'"

"Boys are still terrified of girls who are clever and sexy."

"I think, now, I might have known that would be a complication," said Ivy. "That I'd be a difficult girl to find a man to stand me. People thought I was oversexed. That was my reputation, you see. It was very complicated. And you know how they are. They all hate complications."

"Did you have other boyfriends before Maxim?"

"Yes, I did. In fact I was never quite sure if I was a virgin or not. Maxim and I were having dinner one night in our regular restaurant and I was telling him all about my first boyfriend, and he listened for a bit, and then he said 'I don't understand this story. Why are you telling me all this? Did you sleep together?' Or perhaps, being Russian, he didn't say that, perhaps he just said 'intercourse', or something. It wasn't very apt. And then he looked straight at me, almost like a father, you know. A solid, comforting presence, and asked if I was a virgin.

"I don't know," I said truthfully, "I thought *you'd* know."

"He said he'd never forget my eyes that night in that place. We often talked of it, you know, years afterwards. It was a private joke. He said 'You looked at once so innocent and so cunning'. And it was then that I said to him, 'Oughtn't *you* to know?' And he said, 'I think I do . . .'"

"Read our stars," said Ivy, passing me the morning paper. "I'm going to make the tea."

I stood in her kitchen while she whizzed from sink to stove, opening all the milk bottles for the cream, saving the silver tops for the birds, tearing the wrapping off the biscuit packet. They were very refined biscuits, I remember; those vanilla flavoured thins. "Let's see... Well, Gemini says: 'Friends pass on information which sets you in rapid motion today.' That's you. And Aquarius says: 'Older readers very much on the same wavelength with the younger generation.' That's me."

My tape recorder hiccupped with our laughter.

"You see, it's deadly accurate," said Ivy, handing me my tea. "And all done with computers, nowadays."

14

Adam seemed preoccupied. "What's for dinner?" he asked absently, coming into the kitchen where Sarah and David stood at the cooker wearing identical aprons.

"More supper than dinner," said Sarah apologetically. "And we're having it in here."

David turned a glowing face to his father. "Guess what we're having! My favourites. Bacon and egg and sausages and tomatoes and baked beans."

A scowl of disgust came over Adam's face and he sat down heavily at the kitchen table. "You're dead right. That's not dinner. I can have that at the BBC canteen. What happened to that Cordon Bleu I married?"

"I did it for David," she said.

"Yes. She did it for me. Well, I *asked* her," he said.

"You can say that again," said his mother. "At five minute intervals right through the day."

"I thought I was the boss around here," grumbled Adam, "at least when I'm home. You can pander to him all the time I'm away."

They glared at each other across the table, these two power

struck males of hers, as she plonked sizzling plates down before them and saw to it there was plenty of hot buttered toast.

"It's fattening, too," said Adam miserably, helping himself to the toast, and transferring the hostility of his gaze to Sarah.

Deliberately, David got off his chair. For a moment, Sarah thought, My God, this child is a miracle of sensitivity – he's going to his father! but David came and sat in Sarah's lap, consolidating his win. She found herself wondering whether a girl child would have sat herself in Adam's lap in that well known feminine reflex known as comforting the loser? Probably not. Over the child's head she saw Adam's eyes accuse her: you love him more than you love me. You don't need me, either of you. You're an entity, together.

She had more than enough love for them both, God knew. They didn't, it seemed. How does one show more tender loving care to two such hungry monsters? Not with bacon and eggs.

"Your favourite supper's getting cold," she informed her son. He leapt back onto his seat and attacked the food with all the dedication and vigour of a seasoned trencherman.

"You can see where he gets that from," said Sarah, fondly, glancing at her husband. "You haven't forgotten, I hope. We're going to my mother's tonight. She's been waiting patiently to see you ever since you got back from your last trip."

"I can't," said Adam. "Not tonight." He saw Sarah's face. "Look, you may not have noticed but there's a crisis in television. Redundancies. Strikes. There's a meeting tonight and I have to go to it."

"Christ, Adam, she's counting on it. She's been planning it for weeks. Today would have been their wedding anniversary. I never involve you if I can help it. I try to see her alone. But tonight she needs us to be there."

"I'm unpopular enough as it is," Adam said. "I'm one of the big spenders, I make prime-time, over-budget, prestige programmes. You know my reputation as a slave driver. If I don't show up tonight they'll have my guts for garters."

Sarah stared dismally at him, while the controversial bacon and eggs on her plate grew unappetizingly cold.

"Well, I'll go and telephone," she said.

"Mother, it's me. I'm afraid we can't come tonight. Adam has a meeting . . ."

Her mother's voice went tight and dry and there were tears behind it. "Well, I wish you had let me know," she said. "I could have made other arrangements. Now I'll have to spend the whole evening alone. And you know I can't bear to be alone. Especially – tonight."

"Oh, the birthdays, anniversaries, even Christmases I've had to spend alone when Adam was away or working overtime," Sarah said. "It can't be helped."

"You've got a lot more anniversaries in front of you, I hope, than I have," Dolly said.

An explosion took place inside Sarah then. An explosion in her head, in her gut, in her solar plexus. Shrieking wordlessly, she banged the phone down, grabbed a raincoat, bag, keys. Mouthed "I have to go" at Adam in a tone so high-pitched it may have been silent, and slammed the front door with a violence that resounded through the house.

She dashed into the street, hailed a taxi, and sat in the back of it sobbing and talking to herself incoherently. She stormed into her mother's flat, pushed poor Dolly into the living room and let her have it. For fully five minutes she stood there, shouting and screaming at her mother. Tears poured down her face and she gasped for breath.

"You're a selfish old cow. You turn the screw. I have other commitments. You're full of self-pity. You twist the knife. Don't you know me at all?"

Her mother stood aghast against her "good" velvet furniture, trying to fade into it, but failing.

"You should have let me know," she said doggedly, "It wasn't fair to me."

"To you. To you," shrieked Sarah. "What about being fair to me?"

It was raining heavily outside and she was breathing heavily and crying in a rasping way that hurt her chest.

She walked and walked through the rain, getting wetter but calmer, arguing loudly with herself. "I can manage the mothers quite well when Adam isn't here. I can manage Adam and David and work when the mothers aren't leaning on me. I can't manage all of it, it's too damn much. Well, it would be for anyone, wouldn't it?" She breathed in the cool, wet air and shook herself, like a dog. "I'm like some pathetic rag doll pulled between Adam and Dolly. Being torn to pieces. I always have been, since we first got married. They're so alike, really, Adam and my mother. No wonder each thinks the other selfish and is a little wary. They both behave like children in order to tyrannize and both of them get away with it. They demand. They dominate. Each of them wants me to put them first. I got married too young, I suppose. Do girls who get married while they're still growing up (which means most girls), go readily into situations where their husbands behave to them exactly as their mothers have always behaved to them? It's an old pattern and it reassures. They haven't left home at all. Demands, demands. Grow your hair. Cut your hair. Do this. Do that. Imposing their will. They'll pull me to bits between the two of them. Well, I've grown up, I suppose. I must have done. I cope now in the grown-up world while Adam's away. I make the decisions. I've learned to enjoy it. Then when he comes back he expects me to revert to a docile four-and-a-half year-old again."

Eventually, sodden with rain and self-pity, she hailed a taxi and headed home, expecting a furious Adam who would shout at her: "Now you've done it. How could I go out and leave the child alone?" An Adam mystified: "You've never been irresponsible before." But when she got back the place was in darkness and she stood just inside the front door, listening, sniffing, peering into the shadows. There was no one there. She didn't put on the lights. Still with her coat on, she went into David's room. The familiar smells of coal tar soap and paints and something faintly rubbery rose up to meet her. The bed had not been slept in; the tartan rug which covered it was folded still. She stood for a moment looking out of the window, past the heads of teddy bears and one-eyed woolly animals which crowded the sill. It was raining, still.

She went back into the hall, switched on a lamp and saw the note. "Gone to meeting. Taken David with me. A."

In the half dark of her silent bedroom she stared into the mirror. Was there anyone there she knew?

15

As soon as she got inside Paddington station she began to feel better. She stood for a moment and breathed in that special tarry, smoky, station smell, while David hopped excitedly round her.

"You didn't tell me we were going on a train."

The new high speed engines crouched at the end of the platforms, their powerful yellow noses pointed for the run. The great vaulted glass domes of the place described broader skies. Hustle and bustle and order. Drama and predictability. Meetings and partings. Escape.

They sat in the train like two conspirators facing one another, watching the hands of an enormous clock.

"When it reaches five minutes past, we'll be off," said Sarah.

And they were. The whistle blew, doors slammed, the train moved. They giggled happily. Out of the great glass cathedral they slid, out through the suburbs, picking up speed, settling to rhythm, watching the countryside redefined.

"We're away. I've escaped," thought Sarah, staring through the window. "To a land of green hills and wide skies. Of crops and cattle and cottages and swollen rivers about to burst their banks. Other peoples' problems."

Lovely wodgy white bread sandwiches came round. There were cardboard cups of really hot coffee. She began to relax. David unwrapped a chocolate biscuit and took an experimental lick.

"Where are we going?" he asked.

"To another country," she replied, mysteriously.

His eyes grew larger. "We can't cross the sea on a train."

"We're going west," she said. "Now where can it be?"

David intoned on his chocolatey fingers: "England, Ireland, Scotland and Wales. We're going to Wales!"

"You've got it," she said. "We'll get off the train when it gets into Wales. There'll be green hills and blue mountains and lots of sheep. There'll be a ruined castle on a big wide river estuary. And we'll stay at a pub."

She looked at her son, excited yet composed, taking everything in. Sometimes she thought he was the only grown up person she knew. She felt almost like saying "I've run away. I couldn't take any more." He'd understand. "They can manage without me for a bit. They're all grown up. Or meant to be, anyway."

"Is it different in Wales?"

"You'll see. Let's count the differences you find."

"Smells different, that's one," said David, sniffing the damp coal-tarry air. "Smells Welsh." They passed through the ticket barrier. "Sounds different, too. That's two."

"Wait till you hear them speaking their own language."

"Ooh, there's the castle."

They trudged up a hill and found a place to stay.

"The hills are a different green," said David. "And slate is a bluey mauve. Or a greyish blue. That's four."

"Is it Dafydd, you're called?" asked the lady, setting a plate of shepherd's pie with carrots and leeks and a banger on the side in front of him. "A fine name for a fine young man. Will you be having apple pie to follow? It's all homemade."

"Dafydd," said David faintly. Even with his mouth full you could tell he was impressed. "Do you think that's five?"

"I should think it is," said Sarah, watching him smother the cut up sausage with ketchup and eat it with concentration. She drank a draft lager and looked about her. The place had slate floors and low ceilings. An open fire. A dog. A dog basket. A cat. Dark came with a rush down the hill behind the pub and settled, so you knew there were no more lights, or fires, or human company to be had until tomorrow. The hills closed in, keeping their dark, Celtic secrets green for another day.

"I wonder what Daddy's having for supper," said David.

Before she put him to bed, they leaned out of the window of their tiny bedroom and breathed in the darkness. No stars. No moon.

"You might hear an owl tonight," said Sarah, as she tucked him in. It was a cue for his favourite rhyme:

When I am sleepy in my bed
And birds are sleepy too,
The wise old owl flies overhead
And cries Two Whit, Two Whoo...

"Your usual, Mr Hughes," asked Brenda the barmaid, as

the bar filled up with regulars. How friendly they seemed, these people. How relaxed.

"Seen your picture, haven't I?" asked Brenda. "In one of the magazines. You're a writer, aren't you?"

"Journalist," said Sarah.

"Yes. I've read your stuff about the old ladies. I liked it. You should meet my Gran. You'd like her. She's eighty-five and still going strong. And she's all for women's rights . . ."

A young man with an elf's face and a cat's grace and a head of curly hair came up to the bar.

"There you are, Lloyd," said Brenda, handing him a large gin and tonic. "Here's another writer for you. The place is thick with them tonight."

"David Lloyd," the young man said, and gripped Sarah's hand. "I saw you earlier," he said. "You had your arms round a gorgeous young man. Leading him upstairs she was too." He winked at Brenda. "I'd guess he was – seven?"

She looked at him sharply. He had slanting green eyes like a leprechaun's eyes and had fixed them intently upon her.

"How did you know?"

"I don't know." He shrugged. "I don't have any children, myself, alas. Let's say that I recognized something and the something was me. I only pretend to be adult, don't I, Brenda?"

The young man gave Sarah the strangest sensation. Apart from the eyes, he was David grown up. David with stubble on his determined chin. She shivered.

"And then I saw you and I recognized something else. The perfect couple. Mother and son. You belonged. There you were, 'your arms round the griefs of the ages'."

He grinned and took a swig of his G and T and put his

elbows on the bar in the manner of one at home, and all the time his disturbing eyes transfixed her.

Around him, men discussed the advantages of breeding the long-horned Jacob sheep over other more common breeds, especially in mountain country; a road accident that had happened yesterday and knocked someone's hedges down; the deficiencies of the local sewage system; the possibility that a recent flu virus might have been brucellosis.

"Oh, look," Brenda said, "there are some foreigners come in."

Heads turned. "They're from across the valley. We never see them here. Must be two mile away," she explained.

"A cottage? I can find you a cottage, if you like," the young man was saying. "Or you can stay with me. You can have the whole west wing. I've been rattling around in that place since my wife went, lonely and gone to seed. A prey for all the randy ladies in the district. Other people's wives. But you'd have problems, you know, if you moved here. You'd never be accepted. They won't accept me because I lived in New York for a while, and *I'm* Welsh. I thought I was coming home. I dreamed of this place. But you can't come home again. I've learned that much." He stared into his glass.

"They all want something from you, something you can't give. A part of you, you can't tear out. They want you to solve their problems. It's the old scenario. The Outsider. You know the one. Lone Ranger rides into town. Meets the problems of Little Black Creek head on. Wins some and loses some. Leaves town. Rides on."

"No sunset, mind, just a trail of broken hearts," said Brenda.

"Take Brenda, for example. They've never accepted you,

have they, my lovely? She's a bright girl, and she's had a tough time."

"That big lad over there – that's my son," Brenda said to Sarah. "I had him when I was seventeen. I got knocked up, of course. My mum and dad stood by me, but I'm stuck, you see. Stuck here in the pub, for life. I'm a feminist, too, just like you. And so is my mum. But what can we do?"

"She breaks out now and again, don't you, love?"

"And we hear about it."

"At the time of the full moon . . ."

"She takes all her clothes off, and . . ."

"Belt up, all of you," she said, "or I'll tell on you all, and she'll put it in the magazine. That'll serve you right."

"I do break out," she said to Sarah. "I go mad sometimes. Well, wouldn't you? It's a very small place, you know."

She waved across the bar. "There's Huw . . ."

Huw was a farmer who'd found his wife in bed with his manager and taken a shot gun to them. Fortunately, he'd missed.

"This is Sarah," said David Lloyd. "Meet Huw. He's looking for a wife."

"Who's be a farmer's wife," said Brenda, wrinkling her nose. "He's up to his elbows in gore half the time, midwiving his sheep. Or else he's shearing them so that the pelts come off whole, or something."

"Who'd be a doctor's wife," said the doctor's wife, ordering double Scotches and giving young Lloyd a straight look. "Who're *you*?" she demanded of Sarah.

The colonel had arthritis and the judge had gout and the school teacher dandruff and pomposity. The doctor had his wife. They were all so nice to Sarah (except for the doctor's wife) she could only suppose she was not so much foreign, like the folks from across the valley, but more from outer space.

"I wish I had someone like you down here to talk to," said Brenda wistfully. "I'm sure I could make the break if I could only share my problems. You don't fancy moving, I s'pose?"

"I wish you would," said Lloyd. "Be great for me if you did. I'd be protected from all those home-made apple pies and chutney. Oh, do come down... At least come tomorrow morning and see the place. I'll pick you up from here, and I'll get you back in time to catch the train."

She was fed prawn cocktail and rump steak and rough Beaujolais in the dining room and wheeled back to the bar for a nightcap or two. They were joined by a gentleman tramp who wore gaiters and plus fours and bowed in a courtly fashion. He carried his household in a parcel, neatly done up in brown paper and string, and he, too, had his problems. Amnesia was one of them. Apparently he couldn't remember his earlier life. "Well, Sarah could get him to a hypnotist, couldn't she?" someone said. "The magazine would pay. There'd be a damn fine interview, if you ever got him talking."

Quietly, Sarah crept upstairs to her tiny room, locked the door, and slept.

"Mummy, Mummy, wake up. There's someone outside in a jeep, no a Land Rover, and he's come to pick us up. There's a big brown dog in the back."

"That's no dog," said Lloyd. "That's Barney."

"He looks like you," said David. "You've both got curly brown hair."

They came down the bare mountainside in the Land Rover, passing granite boulders, a waterfall or two, and fording a stream. They passed their first castle, away in the distance, perched on a rocky crag. "There used to be golden eagles in its tower," said Lloyd, "but I haven't seen them for some time. There are larks hanging in the air in early summer. Today we might see a hawk if we are lucky." The sound of water rushing pursued them down the mountain and into the golden valley. Light seemed trapped in the valley. "Merlin's light," said Lloyd. "The sun sets later here than anywhere else in Wales."

David was singing tunelessly to himself: "The grass is greener, the sky is bluer, the river more rivery grey."

Somewhere along the river road, Barney began to growl and a strong smell of dog rose up from the back seat. They turned into a drive overhung with trees, passed a wood and a lawn and a dell, crunched to a stop.

"It's too much for me on my own," explained Lloyd. "There's so much needs doing all the time, and I haven't got all the tools. I'm lucky if I can get the lawn-mower from time to time. It's a pity. This place should be lived in. It's loved all right, but time and attention and money . . . oh, well." He kicked the dry bark of a massive tree trunk lying in the drive. "The centre of this was hollow – and honeycombed, too, by rather ancient bees. So I had to have it felled. And now I shall have to have it moved."

Two donkeys with friendly faces were whining for attention at the paddock gate. David was entranced, though a little nervous.

"They've been waiting for you," said Lloyd. "I told them you were coming. They'll give you a ride. And after that, and after you've explored a bit, there's a swing in the woods and it's on a slope so you seem to be swinging higher than the house. Wait!" He stared very hard at a tree which was quite far away. "Well, that's a good omen," he told them, giving Sarah a strange look. "There's a buzzard in that tree. I must get my binoculars."

"I've prepared you a country breakfast," Lloyd said, later on.

"Well, it's got to be better than the pub."

Thick country-cut bacon, and eggs from his hens, a fresh, brown, crusty loaf, strong, salty Welsh butter.

"There are mushrooms galore. I should have picked you some."

"Did you pick the honeysuckle for the table? Did you put those daisies in that small blue pot?" He had.

She looked around the kitchen they sat in and he caught her look. "Oh, it's damp in here, and cold. And barely converted, I know . . ."

A new Aga, or perhaps an open fire? She'd tile the floor, build in the sink, whitewash the walls. A Welsh dresser'd be perfect and maybe an old oak settle? She stopped herself in the midst of this fantasy.

"Wait till you see the rest," he said. But she already knew what she would see and she wanted it. It was love at first sight. Her heart beat painfully with recognition: here was the house of childhood, the house of dreams. There'd be panelling, peeling off, and lovely old doors, and windows with window seats. There'd be a bathroom, large and cold and an ancient loo, with a rusty chain.

"You can have your own set of rooms, a suite, you see," Lloyd said. "A bedroom, a dressing room, a sitting room with a window seat – once I can get the lintel piece repaired. I'm going to convert the large lavatory into a bathroom and make it all self-contained."

He slept, for the moment, in a small bed in a large damp room, with an old black Bible at his side. And on the Bible, an unmistakable small yellow pill. So there was valium in Paradise. Well, well . . . The Lord was his shepherd. He had brought him to green pastures and made him to lie down by quiet waters, yet Lloyd needed tranquillizers like anyone east of Eden.

Branches knocked against panes, there was moss on the doorstep stones, daisies studded the drive. So much to do! Yet she breathed so easily here. How she longed to take it all over, give it warmth, love and money. And how it would lap them all up, especially the money.

"I need to see children here," said Lloyd, watching David running on the uncut lawn. "Tch! Daisies and dandelions everywhere! Did you know that daisies are the Day's Eye? I wish I could see this place through the eye of childhood."

From the window the river curved silver through the golden valley, the curve of a heart in good working order. Sarah felt sheltered as the house itself was sheltered by its ancient trees. She felt settled, as the house itself was settled in its valley.

"I'm so sick of being here alone," said Lloyd. "It's the kind of place that needs a woman's care."

Not for the proud man apart
From the raging moon, I write.
On these spindrift pages
Nor for the towering dead
With their nightingales and psalms
But for the lovers, their arms
Round the griefs of the ages
Who pay no praise or wages
Nor heed my craft or art.

His voice fitted every word, shaped every phrase.

He looked at Sarah, watching her face as she watched the light change on the mountains.

"Do you get this light show every day?"

He came towards her. "Every day," he said, hands on her shoulders, lips behind her ear.

She turned to face him.

"You're right. There's nothing wrong here that the love of a good woman couldn't cure."

She'd intended a laugh, but he kissed her instead, and his kiss was no laughing matter.

"Oh, Lloyd," she said. "I came down here to run away and now I shall have to run away from you."

"It wasn't *very* different in Wales," said David as they boarded the train for London. "Except for Lloyd of course. And the donkeys."

So much for running away.

16

ENCOUNTERS/ENCOUNTERS

I took Jean Rhys to tea at the Ritz. She was in her early eighties at the time, though none of us knew it. She was still bashful about her age. She made her entrance late, but gracefully, completely kitted-out in the colour of champagne: suit and blouse, shoes and stockings, hat and veil. It was the driest champagne, of course, and the effect was, like the drink, spectacular, so that I didn't notice for quite some time that she wore a wig to match, a mass of champagne curls; and good pearls with that special after-champagne glow. An air of expectant radiance hung about her as she looked round the place, that prettiest of palm courts, positioning herself picturesquely against a pillar, by a potted plant in a fragile golden chair. Who might she meet this afternoon who would buy her the drink she most resembled? She turned her head towards the gentlemen. Well, we would see.

The thing to remember about Jean is that she was always the cocotte. She was still pretty in her eighties, and it was a girlish, rather than a womanly, prettiness. Jean had spent her whole life as a girl. The same girl who had left the warmth and laughter of her father's home in the Caribbean, for cold damp gloomy servitude in England, and had been searching for that early warmth and laughter ever since. Gershwin's *Someone to Watch Over Me* might have been written for Jean. Her eyes still held the beseeching, please-help-me look of that "little lamb who's lost in the wood". She had enormous eyes, a pale somewhat watery blue, and there was something about the set of them and the way she rolled them towards heaven sometimes, in what must once have been her "roguish" look, which made me wonder if she had mixed blood? No wonder she shivered in the dank basements or those Bloomsbury bedsits. No wonder she was so beady and professional about her work. There is no evidence for my suspicion in the family background. The good Welsh doctor, her father, knew all the answers once, long ago and faraway. And she was still his daughter. His pretty, talented daughter, his little girl, who prayed every day "Oh God, let me be pretty when I grow up. Let me be, let me be," her voice lisping slightly, her manner, impish or coy, her body slender as an adolescent's. She must have been a sadist's dream, Jean one moment full of mischief and retort, the next cowering to be hit. That she was eighty-four going on seventeen was no surprise. She would always be seventeen, age of her exile from the sunlit splendours of the Caribbean when she had been condemned to a life of unremitting chill, and a job in the theatre as a chorus girl, an unsuccessful chorus girl, of course. Provincial theatres, smelly digs, landlady trouble, gentleman trouble, no-gentleman-he trouble. No success. No money. No sunlight.

Jean had been "designed" to get a man to keep her. She married three times, yet somehow failed as a kept woman every time. She suffered rejection, poverty, abortion, the death of a child, loneliness, melancholy. She suffered failure, success, eclipse, revival, respect. Only in her relationship with her work did she show a cold, hard eye, and a toughness of mind and spirit. The blank page was her mirror of truth, and, faced with it, she could be as fierce, as demanding, as any writer. "Mirror, mirror on the wall, who is the victim of them all?" Staring, she saw only herself, distraught, as usual. So, when "He" had gone, the last impossible he, when the gloomy bedsit loomed again and the cheap carafe awaited, the feint ruled page would save her. Pretty little victim became clever little victim, spilling bitterness, wit, unvoluntary cravings, on that page, observing her own passivity, discovering steel inside her which could etch words sharply, discovering acid, which burned indelibly. This is what Jean had that the women she wrote about didn't have. She had the work. She had the words. She could draw pictures with them. In early Hockney style, perhaps. A window open on a narrow street, a bed crumpled, a bed empty, a room disordered, a woman waiting. She could describe with them: herself as victim. The man as heel. He said and she said and he said. The hopelessness of it all.

A lot of this took place in Paris and

seemed very French. The best reporters like to report from the front,and the front, just then, was Paris. There were other women there who resembled Jean, superficially, at least. Strong with the pen, weak with the men. Colette, for instance, at the period when she posed for those naughty pix: suggestive sphinxes and other fantasies. Colette, who married twice before she met and married a younger, safer, man.

Jean had gone to France in the first place to write fairy tales for a rich lady, who lived on the Riviera. There was always trouble. With husbands, with wives, with the friends of husbands and the friends of wives. She was always the third partner in the marriage, she was always asked to leave, she had always (unwittingly?) caused the trouble.

In Paris she met a genuine patron, Ford Madox Ford. In Paris she met genuine café life, genuine French squalor, genuine loneliness. No one could bring her velvety nights, or sounds of carnival. Or warmth. Sometimes she fell willingly into someone's arms: they had promised to keep her warm. She was always shivering, Jean, even in clear spring sunshine, even when wrapped in furs.

About Paris she wrote the *Left Bank* stories (1927), *Quartet* (1928), *After Leaving Mr. Mackenzie* (1930), *Good Morning Midnight* (1939). After the revival caused by *Wild Sargasso Sea* in the late sixties, Jean held court from time to time at the Portobello, an elegant small hotel in a crumbling part of Kensington, escaping her ugly bungalow in Devon with relief. Journalists called, homage was paid, students and admirers sought her out, fan mail arrived, she was photographed, fêted and fed. And yet, when the circus departed she was not merely left alone, she was abandoned. The image sticks: two chairs at a Paris café table. One empty. In the other, a girl, hunched into her coat. Two glasses on the table, both full. She drinks alone.

I visited Jean in hospital. A harsh spotlight over the bed lit up her hair which seemed impossibly white and soft and flowed round her head as a halo might. It was very flattering, but there was nothing saintly about Jean.

"You look marvellous," I said to her. "I don't know what they've got you in for, but you don't need any of it – except the rest."

She glowed mischievously at me.

"There you are in all that cruel light and it reveals nothing but radiance. I'm jealous," I said. And I was. "I wouldn't like to get under that light and receive gentlemen at the bedside," I told her. "And I dare say I'm younger than you."

She was pleased at that. Her smile became shy and impish again and her voice took on the remembered girlish lilt, though the light quaver in it sat oddly with her sprightly manner.

"Well," she said, whispering conspiratorially, "well. I rely a lot on make-up, you know. Oh, yes, I do . . ."

The lines on Jean's face were passive lines: subservience, complacency, acceptance, a woman done to rather than doing, who had smiled and smiled while she was being done. Alone among the Fast Ladies, I have not noted a ribald laugh, a survivor's laugh. Jean did not laugh. She was not a survivor. Jean was a victim, who smiled her haunted, camellia-scented smile. Sometimes, it is the victim who survives.

"Why do I always imagine things will get better?" Sarah asked Mel.

"Aquarians are optimists," said Mel, who was up a ladder

sloshing paint of a peculiarly dingy mushroom colour on a wall. She was working, nowadays, at a kindergarten and studying child psychology at night. It seemed to have given her energy.

"Is there another brush?" Sarah asked. "I suppose I could help you with that."

"You'd better do it well," Mel warned her, "this is very expensive, specially mixed paint." She observed her handiwork with pleasure. "You can see that from the colour. Subtle, isn't it?"

Sarah retrieved a brush and butcher's apron from the garden shed and returned.

"Things don't get better," she said, trying to keep her brush strokes even and not to drip the paint. "They get worse and worse. People get steadily older. They get ill. They die. I used to look forward to things. Didn't you? Like Victorians, you know, brought up to believe life was progressive. Early struggles would be rewarded. Success arrived late at the party, and stayed."

"You're a very frightened lady," Mel said.

There was a pause while Sarah's arm froze in shock and mushroom paint dripped over the newly sanded and polished floor, neatly missing the newspapers spread around.

"If anyone else but you had said that, I'd have emptied that bucket of paint on their head," said Sarah. "What am I frightened of?"

"Come on, Sarah! The example of your mother's and Adela's weakness scares you silly. You're so determined to be strong yourself in all circumstances, to be in control, to be independent. The idea that you – Sarah the strong – may one day be reduced to dependency yourself terrifies you." Mel paused and sat down on the top rung of the ladder. "It must be because you don't trust anyone else to look after you. You think they'd let you down.

"In our child psychology programme we learn that people grow up by testing their strength gradually. A baby learns to stand up by a series of falls."

"I was also very dependent on parental approval, you know. The old one: no approval, no love. Be good, sweet maid . . ."

"And let who will be clever," Mel finished. "My best friend in Lower III wrote that in my autograph book. I went off her after that."

"I was quite incapable of making decisions. I emerged so bloody slowly it was painful. When I got married I simply replaced my mother's domination by my husband's domination. Pathetic! It's taken me so long to be me, I must be terrified, I suppose, of being sucked down again."

"That's why you so badly needed the Fast Ladies to be strong. You craved examples that were not like Dolly or Adela. You wanted to believe it was possible to grow old, or ill, or even to die, without fear. But of course the old ladies were only human. They were strong and weak in turn, like everyone else."

"Yes, inside every one of those old women was a frightened child, a romantic girl, a disillusioned wife. People don't change as they grow old, they go on being the person they have always been. They're often stuck at a certain point in their development."

"I liked what you said in your introduction to the series. What was it? Something about 'Our mothers' generation having ruined their lives by trying to live vicariously, through their husbands or their children'."

"And our generation ruining our lives by trying not to . . ."

"The truth is, no one can cope with these things: old age, illness, loneliness, death. The only thing that helps at all is having lived. Having *loved*. No one can bear the unbearable. When things happen to us, we bear what we have to bear, that's all. Survival – like birth or death – is often an accident."

"But people bear things according to character," Sarah said. "The Fast Ladies seemed strong characters. But they were all doomed, or baffled, like the rest of us. I wanted them to rage."

"Rage, rage against the dying of the light," declaimed Mel, taking up her brush again. "It's you who are in a rage, my love."

Sarah slopped paint on wearily, bending the brush this way and that. "There's never anyone to lean on," she said. "The mothers took out insurance against old age and loneliness. It was called marriage. It meant that you were secure. And look at them now. The Fast Ladies weren't pillars of strength after all. I needed them to survive. At the rate I'm going I'm not sure I'll survive. I thought I could hang on to them as examples. They'd all been through more – or worse – than I have."

"They're only people, heroines. Even heroes are only people. They do what they can."

"I don't want to grow up. I want to regress."

"Maybe one day you'll meet someone who'll look after you. Without undermining your strength."

"Now who's the optimist," said Sarah.

17

Sarah went with Adam to a special screening of the African programme at the television centre. It was a pretty hard-hitting programme Adam had made, showing things as they are among emerging African nations, and the top brass were supposed to estimate the risks of showing it. From the first frame the story was told with the kind of authority you cannot ignore. There were real problems on the screen – or in your sitting room – anomalies, bitterness, humour. Shots of grinning soldiers brandishing brand new Kalashnikov rifles. Representations would surely be made by the government in question. How could the television company show members of that government the programme in advance and still preserve their integrity? And how could they show the programme to the public if they didn't? Adam had given them a problem. Arguments broke out in the "Senior Common Room". The one person who remained cool was Adam. He seemed to know exactly what he was doing, exactly how far he could go. He amazed her. He told stories and jokes over the drinks. He defused arguments. She heard tales she had never heard before about an Adam she had never met.

While he was shooting the programme in Africa, he had needed some extras from a local tribe to recreate a scene of a hundred years before when the region had been "discovered" by English explorers. Imagine his dismay when they all turned up in chain store trousers and shirts, when what he needed were loin cloths and skins. He conferred with the Chief of the tribe, who conferred with the men, who said "no, suh" on no account would they wear the loin cloths and skins of ancient times. The Chieftain even went to the market with a fistful of television money, and bought the skins, hoping to persuade the men to wear them, but the "natives" refused. Independence had really got through to them.

Adam got into his jeep with the Chieftain and drove up to the District Commissioner's residence. Palladian columns gleamed white in the sunshine. The Rolls convertible in the drive gleamed scarlet. The DC's skin was a polished blue black plum and his teeth a polished ivory.

"Come in, old boy," he said, turning down the volume on Vivaldi's *Four Seasons* which was relayed at concert pitch throughout the house. "What'll you have? G and T? Or are you for Scotch?"

The Chieftain stood uneasily to attention and the DC waved him to a chair, where he sat, silent and out of place. The drinks clinked agreeably in their glasses. The room was cool. Adam became aware of his dust-covered denims as he surveyed the creases in the DC's white sharkskin suit. "I think I recognize you," the DC said, his face like ebony, gleaming in the shadows. "You *are* an Oxford chap? Which college?"

How Adam wished he was Professor Higgins so that

he could just look at the DC and declare: Marlborough, Sandhurst, Oxford, Stanford and LSE. The DC's accent was clearer than the cut glass crystal tumblers they drank from.

The supremacy of Oxford once established, they swopped stories about undergraduate days, while the Chieftain smiled and nodded in bewilderment, almost forgotten in his corner.

"Well, then, old boy, what seems to be the trouble?"

"I was so disarmed by this time, I almost said: having a little trouble with the natives, but I managed to put it a little more tactfully than that."

"Oh, I'll talk to them," the DC said. "They don't understand the concept of history, you see. The fact that your film is set in the past means nothing to them. 'The past is another country,' eh, old boy? Leave it to me."

He went over to the Chieftain and put a heavy hand on the poor man's shoulder and spoke to him like a father, though the Chief was many years the DC's senior. They spoke in their own language, but Adam got the gist of it: "Don't worry. I'll talk to them. No harm can come of it. This man's a friend."

Thus were the loin cloths won.

"Honestly, Adam," Sarah said later. "You never tell me things."

"I can't remember everything that happens when we're filming. Besides, if I did tell you, most of the time you'd only worry."

True. She was used to hearing months later of jeeps that had overturned and helicopters which had crashed. Once a ski-plane had deposited Adam on the side of some glacier and left him there alone with his view-finder. How had he been sure they would locate him to pick him up again?

Once, he'd made the whole crew follow his example and eat monkeys roasted on spits. "They looked just like babies, roasting," one of the crew had told Sarah. "They were just the same size. We thought we'd discovered cannibals. We didn't want to eat them. "It's all in the job," said Adam. "You boys have got no guts."

Once they were charged from behind by a rhino while getting a shot. This story had been around a bit. One supposes the rhino was some way away. "There's a rhino behind us" said the camera operator. "He's going to charge."

"Yes. I'll just get this shot," said Adam.

Sarah felt curiously hurt that he did not share these adventures with her; didn't he know how totally with him she felt, how completely on his side? Especially on occasions like these when he was under attack. She felt their solidarity as a couple in a way she had not done since they were very young. She remembered with sudden vividness how they had felt then: the world was ganged up against them, but it did not matter: they were together.

At the same time as the controversy about the African programme, Adam was collecting awards for some programmes he had made in America the year before, and setting up an ambitious three year project in South America in case the Hollywood deal fell through. Never satisfied, however much praise he got, that his programmes were as good or as truthful as they might be, he gave Sarah to understand that this time the conditions were going to guarantee him freedom and that this time he was going to try "really hard". "This could be the best thing I've done," he told her, with that boyish lopsided grin of his.

"You mean *this* could be important!"

"Oh, shut up," he said fondly. "You know me much too well. I must say I don't feel myself since I came back from Africa. I'm tired all the time. Must be old age creeping on." A slightly puzzled look crossed his face as he said this, turning quickly to outrage. "Do you know, I felt breathless belting up the stairs at the TV centre yesterday? I actually had to stop! There were pains in my chest."

"I was always afraid you'd catch bilharzia. Some of the crew did, didn't they?"

"What, old Bill and Harry? Don't be silly. It's not that."

"Well, it's hardly surprising you're tired," Sarah said, "When I see the pace you go at all the time. And all that travelling and change of temperature and altitude. Perhaps you should have a check-up, a really thorough one, to set our minds at rest."

"I've got to have one anyway before they'll give me the South American job. They want to know I'll last the course."

So Adam had a two-day check-up and was pronounced fit and healthy on all fronts. He sent the hospital champagne.

"They said the tiredness was due to stress," he said.

"Well, at least it's not some virus you've picked up."

"Of course it's not. They did the tests. I'm in a stressful job. But I'm still tired."

Sarah got loads of lovely coloured leaflets and holiday bumpf. "It says here Lake Como was used by the Romans to restore them to health and tranquillity after the excesses of empire."

"Then Como it is," Adam said.

Meanwhile, he and Sarah got themselves dressed up and grinned into cameras and had themselves described by the "How do you Manage It?" brigade as The Golden Couple, and The Beautiful People, and The Marriage that Works. David loved it, of course. He watched them getting dressed, scrutinizing Adam's cuff-links and bow ties, criticizing his mother's dress – "I can see through it" – and make-up – "You've got too much lipstick on". Trying to brush her hair out of curl so that it would be more the way he liked it. Then he lined them up before the front door as they were going out and pretended to photograph them. His glamorous parents.

"My parents are famous," he told the boys at school.

"Yeah! Prove it!"

"They had their picture in the papers."

Surveying their picture in the paper one morning Sarah said: "You're getting better looking as you get older, Adam. Like your father did. He was really handsome as an old man. I can see just what's going to happen at future premières; you'll look younger and younger and I'll look older and older and they'll photograph you with some young bird on your arm instead of me."

"Oh, nonsense," said Adam, lightly touching the top of her head. "You'll always be the baby."

Not long after these events the "golden couple" were sitting close together on the sofa watching a re-run of Hitchcock's *Marnie* on Adam's new video-tape machine.

"Never was much good at the psychology, the old boy," Adam said, after a particularly banal line, then he gulped, and a few seconds later she felt his arm fly out and hit her side.

"Hey, darling," she said. "That hurt."

She pulled away and looked at him, then got quickly off the sofa and stared at him. He looked healthy enough. His colour was high and his eyes very bright, but he stared straight ahead without speaking and his limbs jerked rhythmically from side to side.

Then his head repeated the movement, jerking steadily from left to right.

"Darling, what's the matter?" she said in alarm, grabbing a cushion and trying to prop up his head with it.

"It's all right. It's all right. You wait here and I'll call the doctor."

"It's me, Mrs Cornish," she screamed, panting into the telephone. "Please come. Come quickly. You've got to come. He's having a stroke. Or a heart attack." What if he could hear her? "Hurry, please hurry. What? He's jerking from side to side. Yes. Yes."

With the greatest difficulty she repeated the address, rushed back to the sofa, watched over him. The jerking went on for some time. She paced about from window to door, more afraid when she was not watching him than when she was. She went back to the telephone and dialled 999. "I need an ambulance," she said, and gave the address and their name. "How long will it take them to get here? Which hospital? Please hurry. It's urgent," she said. She went back to the sofa and saw that his colour had changed. The vividness had subsided, he was much paler now, and the jerks seemed to be coming more slowly. They threw his whole heavy body from side to side.

"It's all right darling," she said, standing in front of him, reassuring. We'll get you to hospital. It'll be all right. They'll make you better. What is it, darling, what's the matter?"

She wondered if he could hear her, see her, if he knew anything at all of what was happening. She hoped not. She thought: he lost consciousness with that ordinary little gulp.

She paced the room and watched, and caressed him continuously with her voice, her eyes. Then the jerks stopped and his body slumped to one side, his head dropping sideways to his shoulder, presenting her favourite face to her: the one she had fallen in love with, while still sixteen. That long, pale, sensitive, half-profile; those blue eyes and heavy straight fair lashes. The beautifully shaped ears. "I have to tuck my ear in" he'd say at night, if the bedclothes had slipped. He couldn't sleep unless his ears were warm. His skin had gone paler still now, and his lips seemed darker. The movements had stopped. He sprawled on the sofa. Still.

"Oh, good," she said, fondly. "Those horrid jerks have stopped. As soon as we get you to hospital, they'll wake you up."

His eyes were open, and blue as ever, but they did not look at her. Instead, she looked at him harder than she had ever done, willing him to be all right, to be with her, to be well. And as she watched, one tear appeared in his eye, welled up, and, perfectly formed, traced its way from his eye and the curve underneath the eye down his cheek, and was lost. One tear. It left no trace at all.

Window, door, once round the sofa again. Did she dare to leave him a second and go down to the street? Could she will the doctor to be quicker? "Don't worry, darling," she repeated. "I'll never leave you."

All this took about twenty minutes, every one of which

lasted an hour. It was only in the last three or four of these that she began to realize what she was watching. She was watching him die.